Fatal Flaw

By Sterling Kirkland

This is a work of fiction. All of the characters, organizations, and events portrayed in this novel are either products of the author's imagination or are used fictitiously.

Fatal Flaw Copyright © 2023 Sterling Kirkland
All rights reserved. Printed in the United States of America.

No part of this publication may be reproduced, stored in a retrieval system, or transmitted in any form or by any means, electronic, mechanical, photocopy, recording, or otherwise, without written permission from the author except brief quotations credited to the author.

ISBN- 9798390171776

Cover designed by GetCovers

Dedicated to all my Facebook fans.

Fatal Flaw

Chapter 1

"Looking at your watch every five minutes isn't going to speed this process up."

Sam dropped her arm, then nodded in agreement. It wasn't like she had the ability to leave the crime scene. Until the remains were removed, she was stuck. For Sam, the worst part was waiting. Hours had passed and she was no closer to learning who the victim was than when she had arrived.

Deep down, Sam knew the crime scene analyst wasn't dragging her feet just for the sake of it. Collecting evidence took time. It was also the most crucial step in the process. The tiniest piece of evidence could make or break a case.

"Any idea if it's a man or a woman?" Sam asked, staring at the skeleton.

"Off the record?" Bobbi asked, taking a long hard look at Sam. "Based on the pelvis bone, I'd say it's a guy, but don't quote me on that."

At least that narrows it down a bit, Sam thought. According to what she had found, the small home hadn't been lived in for more than twenty years. It was only by sheer luck that the skeleton had been discovered. If the community center hadn't been using the home for extra storage, they may have never found it.

"Can you tell how long it's been here?"

Bobbi sat the camera down and gave Sam a stern look. "Do you want me to finish what I'm doing or answer your questions? I can't do both."

Turning around, Sam walked outside, wondering what she had done in a previous life to warrant her current circumstances. For what felt like the hundredth time, she checked her phone. There were still no calls or texts from Gary.

After she texted to let him know that a body had

been discovered at the community center, it had been radio silence. Part of her had expected the man to show up wanting to lend a hand.

Stop. Sam told herself. Killing someone and shoving the body underneath the floor of an abandoned house wasn't a federal crime. Special Agent Gary White had no reason to come to the scene. His presence would have only created additional paperwork for the both of them.

Tucking the phone back into her pocket, she began pacing, wishing that Bobbi would hurry up and find something that would blow the case wide open. It was a pipe dream, and Sam knew it. Very few cases were closed within minutes of finding the body.

With nothing else to do, Sam walked over to the command tent and spoke with Sergeant McMasters. Like always, he had given her a hard time about having to work the crime scene. In his opinion, Sam was the reason why they all had so little free time to enjoy their lives.

"Don't tell me that you found another one," he said, as she approached.

"Not yet, but the night's still young." Sam sat down in one of the folding chairs and sighed. "What am I going to do, Sarge?"

"Figure out who the victim is, then find out why they were killed."

Sam rolled her eyes. "That's not what I mean, and you know it."

Under normal circumstances, Sam would have enjoyed his good-natured ribbing. But her mind was focused on something else. Although she knew there was no way that she could get involved with a federal agent, that's what she wanted to do.

It was McMasters turn to roll his eyes. "Don't you have more important things to worry about than why your date hasn't called you back? In case you've forgotten, this is an active crime scene and you're a police detective."

"Until Bobbi decides that she's done, there's nothing for me to investigate. I've already pulled the property records, the place has been empty for decades. According to the guy who runs the community center, no one's ever broken in or vandalized the place. So there's nothing for me to do until we ID the body."

The two were still discussing what might have happened when a white cargo van pulled into the parking lot. Both turned at the same time, watching the occupants as they exited the vehicle.

Sam glanced down at her watch. "It's about time," she said, as the small group walked toward them.

The anthropologist introduced himself, then the members of his team. Once they were signed in, Sam led the group to the small home. Crossing the threshold, she called out to Bobbi. Like all crime scenes, the analyst was in charge and got to decide who came in and who didn't.

"Dr. Michaels," she said, extending a hand toward the anthropologist, "it's nice to see you again. Sorry to call you out so late, but this falls under your expertise, not mine."

"No worries," the doctor replied. "Always happy to help out the police."

The pair were still exchanging pleasantries when Sam spotted the evidence bags lying on the floor next to Bobbie's kit.

"Did you find something we can use?"

"As a matter of fact, I did," the crime analyst said. "I recovered two bone pins, along with some scraps of what I believe used to be blue jeans."

"What are bone pins?" Sam asked. For the first time in hours, she felt like something other than a spectator. With evidence in hand, she could begin her investigation.

"They're placed inside the body to keep the bones together. In this case, the victim had been in some kind of accident prior to his death. His femur had been fractured in a couple of different places."

"Please tell me that you can track down who put them in or at least who made them."

"I can't, but the M.E. can. I've already sent him the images." Bobbi held up a finger to keep Sam from saying anything. "There's more. I believe there's a wallet underneath the victim."

Chapter 2

Sam pulled the driver's license from the wallet, noting that it expired in nineteen ninety-nine. After taking several photographs of it, she called dispatch and asked them to run the name. A minute later, she was informed that the young man had been reported missing in July of that same year.

This is going to be fun, Sam thought. Solving any murder was hard. One that was twenty-four years old was going to be darn near impossible.

As Bobbi gathered up the additional evidence bags, Sam asked her if she remembered hearing anything about the young man.

The crime scene analyst paused, then nodded her

head. "I remember my parents not letting me go anywhere for a few weeks after he disappeared. At the time, everyone assumed some random nutjob had come to town and either took him or killed him. Then a few weeks later, the story kind of died."

"Thanks." Sam dropped the wallet into an evidence bag and handed it to the analyst. "How long do you think it will take you to get everything packed up?"

"Give us a half an hour."

Leaving them to finish their job, Sam marched over to the command tent to ask Sergeant McMasters about the young man. While she didn't expect him to remember the details, he was one of only two cops left in the department who had been working at the time of the disappearance.

"I haven't heard that name in years," McMasters said, sitting his coffee on the table. "I remember the case well. He went missing on the fourth of July. He was last seen with some friends at Silver Lake. We dragged that lake three or four times looking for him."

"You thought he drowned?"

"At the time, we didn't know what had happened to

him, but it made sense to think he had gone into the lake. All of them had been drinking that night." The sergeant shook his head. "If I remember correctly, a couple of weeks later, we were told the kid left town. Someone said he was either in Phoenix or Albuquerque. Somewhere down there in the desert."

While Sam thought it was odd that they would give up looking for the kid based on someone saying he left, she wanted to reserve judgment until after she looked at the file. It was possible that the report of him leaving town was credible, and without any evidence contradicting the statement, any cop would have moved on to another case. That was the thing about police work, there was always another case which needed your attention.

Hopping into her unmarked Ford Explorer, Sam called Jenna and gave her a quick update. She wanted the sergeant to have James pull up the file while she was at the medical examiner's office. If luck was on her side, whoever the original detective was, had included a list of potential suspects for her to chase down.

"I'll see what I can do," Jenna replied. "Are we sure this is Aaron Burwell?"

"As sure as I can be," Sam answered. "The wallet was underneath what was left of the body. Plus, the missing person's report stated that he walked with a limp. Bobbi found a couple of bone screws."

There was a long pause before Jenna spoke again. When she did, she asked Sam not to speak to the parents until the medical examiner had a chance to look at the implants. "It's been twenty-four years. Another few hours won't make a difference," she said.

Sam agreed. There was no reason to wake the parents up in the middle of the night just to let them know that they might have found their son, or what was left of him.

After hanging up, Sam walked back over to speak with Sergeant McMasters. He had already begun to break down the command tent. While the home would continue to be secured for a few days, the scene was no longer considered active.

"You wouldn't happen to remember who was in charge of the Burwell case, would you?"

McMasters shook his head. "We didn't have any detectives back then, so it would have been handled by one of the patrol sergeants." He stopped and rubbed his chin. "If I had to guess, it was either Edwards or what's his name…" A second later, he snapped his fingers. "Dave Tucker."

Sam prayed it was Tucker. Although it had been more than a year since she had laid eyes on Sgt. Edwards, she was willing to bet the man still carried a grudge against her. She was the reason he was working as a mall security guard instead of as a police detective.

As the memory of their last encounter replayed in her mind, the voice in the back of her head told her to get over it. The victim deserved to get justice. If that meant questioning a former bad cop, so be it.

"Thanks," Sam said. As she turned to leave, another thought popped into her mind. "Do you remember if this Burwell kid ever caused any problems?"

"Not that I can recall. The only time I can remember seeing him was right after his accident. He got hit by a car on his way from work. Busted his leg up pretty good. At the time, we all assumed it was a drunk driver, but as far as I know, we never found the person who hit him."

Thanking the sergeant, Sam headed back to her

SUV. A hundred questions were floating around inside her head, beginning with checking out Aaron's other accident. While it was a long shot, she couldn't stop herself from wondering if the two incidents weren't connected.

Maybe Aaron figured out who ran him over and the person wanted to prevent him from saying anything. And maybe the moon is made out of blue cheese.

Shaking the thought out of her head, Sam started her Ford and waited for the crime scene analyst to finish packing up her equipment.

Chapter 3

"No doubt about it," the medical examiner said, putting the two x rays' side by side. "This is Aaron Burwell." He pointed to the image on the left. "This was taken right after his surgery. See this fracture here."

Although Sam was no expert, she could tell the wound was the same in both images. "Where did you get that?" she asked.

"A few years back, a body was pulled out of Silver Lake. Since we weren't sure who it was, we asked Aaron's family for his medical records. I'll run the DNA just to make sure, but there's no doubt in my mind that this is him."

"Can you tell me what killed him?" Sam asked,

thinking it would be darn near impossible to figure it out.

The M.E. led her over to the table and pointed out several fractures on the spine, before turning his attention to the ribs. "As you can see, several of them are broken off at the ends. Someone beat this kid to death using a blunt instrument like a baseball bat. I'll have to take some measurements, but I've seen enough of these injuries to know what happens when someone is hit with one."

"Thanks," Sam said, tapping her body camera to shut it off. Shoving it into her purse, she jotted a few more things down in her notebook before saying goodbye.

While Sam would have to wait a few weeks or longer to get the final results, she was confident that there was enough proof to move forward in her investigation.

On her way out, she stopped to look at the evidence bags lying on the counter. They all contained bone fragments. She didn't envy the medical examiner. Although he was sure who the victim was, he'd still have to put all the pieces back together before his job was finished.

With her curiosity satisfied, Sam exited the room and called Jenna again. As requested, the sergeant had the other detective pull everything on the case.

"Just don't get your hopes up," Jenna said. "There isn't a lot here. From what I read, it doesn't look like Edwards did much more than talk with the victim's family and friends."

"Of course not." Sam wasn't surprised. While she only interacted with the man a few times, she knew what kind of cop he had been. "No mention of any suspects?"

"As far as Edwards was concerned, the kid left town of his own accord." Jenna paused. "To be fair, there wasn't a lot of evidence that anything had happened to him."

Sam thanked her, then told her that she'd be back at the station soon.

Feeling like she didn't have any other option, Sam called Carol Grasso. The former assistant district attorney from Essex County, New Jersey had a knack for finding out information that others had no prayer of uncovering.

"How was your date?" Carol asked, sounding a lot

like the girls Sam had gone to high school with.

"It never happened," Sam replied. Then she filled the former prosecutor in on what happened. She wasn't sure what the woman could do to help, but she was willing to try anything.

"I'm not sure how much help I can be on this one," Carol said. "Most of the wise guys who were working here at the time are gone now. Are you thinking this kid was taken out by a pro?"

"I don't think so. The M.E. thinks he was beaten to death."

"If it's not something they can pin on the family, why are you worried about it?"

Sam had to bite her lip to keep from screaming at the woman. After counting to ten, she explained that her work consisted of more than keeping the family out of prison.

"I get it," Carol said, cutting her off. "What do you want me to do?"

For a minute, Sam didn't know what to say. In spite of everything, she knew her family and those closest to it would be unable to assist her in closing the case. It wasn't like any of them owned a time machine and could travel back in time to be at the crime scene when the body had been placed there. Feeling like crap, Sam apologized, then asked Carol to forget about the call.

"I'm not saying we're unwilling to help, but none of us were here when this kid went missing. If you had a suspect in mind, that'd be different, but we're not detectives."

"I know." Sam ran a hand over her face as she considered her next move.

In the four years since she had become a cop, Sam had always relied on her family for help. Whether it was providing her with evidence or forcing someone to confess, they were always there to lend a hand. Now she was all alone. If this case got solved, it would be done by old fashioned police work. Something Sam wasn't sure she was capable of.

"I do have one idea, but you're not going to like it."

"What is it?" Sam asked, before she could stop herself. Knowing Carol, it could be anything. The woman had a penchant for framing innocent people.

"There's a federal agent I know who specializes in

closing cold cases. If I didn't know any better, I'd swear the woman was a psychic or something."

"No thanks." The last thing Sam needed in her life was another federal agent. She already had one too many in her opinion. "I'll figure this out on my own."

"She's not associated with the family," Carol said, as if that mattered. "I worked with her several times. She's really good at what she does."

"I appreciate it, but I don't need the feds coming in here and trying to pin this on my dad."

"First of all, that's not what this woman does. Second, your father wasn't operating on the west coast when this guy went missing."

"When has that ever stopped them?" Sam asked. Her frustration level was growing by the second, and she knew that if she didn't get off the phone soon, she'd end up saying something that she'd regret. "Again, I appreciate the offer, but I'd rather not ask the feds for help."

"Have it your way," Carol replied. "If you change your mind, you know how to reach me."

Chapter 4

Sam read the file again, wondering why any cop, even a bad one, would refuse to speak with anyone other than the friends and family of the person who had gone missing. From what she had read, there was no indication that Edwards had spoken to the people who worked at the lake or anyone else for that matter.

This is why so many cases go unsolved, she thought.

Knowing it wouldn't do any good, Sam pulled up the map of the area and jotted down the names of the businesses surrounding the lake. Her plan was to start working the case as if the victim had just gone missing. She'd interview anyone who was still in the area, then work her way outwards to the gas stations and other convenient stores.

Someone had to have seen something, she told herself.

Opening up a new file, Sam typed in everything she knew about the victim. When she was finished, she cursed the former sergeant for being such a lousy cop.

"How's it going?" Amy asked, taking a seat next to Sam's desk. "I heard you caught a tough one."

"That's an understatement." Sam held up her hands as a show that she didn't mean to sound so cold. "I was still in diapers when this guy went missing."

Amy leaned over and looked at the computer screen. "Doesn't look like Edwards did you any favors. Is that all there is?"

"He didn't even talk to the people who worked at the boat launch." Sam pushed herself away from the desk. She wasn't looking forward to what she had to do. "I better let the family know we found him."

"Want me to come with you?"

"No thanks. You've already got enough on your plate." Sam shut down the computer, then grabbed her stuff.

After letting Jenna know that she was off to meet with the family, she exited the building and headed toward the crime lab, which occupied the rear of the property.

Like always, Bobbi was at her desk reviewing photographs. It seemed like that was all she did when she wasn't in the field.

"I hate to bother you, but I was wondering if you've had a chance to look at any of the stuff you collected at the scene?"

The crime scene analyst nodded as she rubbed her eyes. "I'm not finished yet, but I can give you the highlights. We recovered several inches of denim, which we believe came from a pair of jeans. It'll be a while before we find out if the blood we pulled from it belonged to your victim or not, but the odds are, it did. We also sifted through the dirt but weren't able to find the missing teeth."

That didn't surprise Sam. She had suspected the small house was the dump site and not the scene of the killing.

Bobbi held up a file. "This is the initial observation from Dr. Michaels. Nothing official yet, but he feels pretty confident that the vic was beaten to death with a blunt object."

"Like a baseball bat?" Sam asked, remembering the medical examiner's hypothesis.

"Yep. He also thinks that someone came back later and disturbed the body." Bobbi pulled up a series of images that she had taken at the scene. "While it's within the realm of possibility that an animal had discovered the body while it was decomposing, the odds are slim. See these bones? They should be over here."

Sam estimated the distance was only about a foot. "Maybe the body fell over."

"It did," Bobbi said. "Whoever dumped the body let it drop on its left side. Over time, as the body bloated, it fell onto its back. But that doesn't explain why these bones are lying over here. The only way for them to get there was if someone picked the body up after it had decomposed."

The thought sent a shiver up Sam's back. She

couldn't imagine why anyone would disturb the body after it had already decomposed.

As if reading her mind, Bobbi explained that there could only be a couple of reasons as to why someone would go back. They either needed to remove the victim's clothing, which she didn't believe, or they wanted something that was on the victim, like a ring, watch or bracelet.

A watch made the most sense given that Aaron was eighteen at the time of his death. Sam couldn't picture someone fresh out of high school wearing a bracelet or ring.

"Thanks," Sam said, as she turned to leave.

When she got outside, she thought about the type of person who would go back and disturb a corpse. In her mind, it had to be someone who was desperate.

But why? Sam asked herself. *Unless the watch or whatever the victim had on his person when he was killed was a gift given to him by the killer, there'd be no way to trace it back to the person who killed him.* Then another thought entered her mind. *Maybe Aaron fought back, and the perp thought they had been scratched by the watch.*

Although neither scenario seemed likely, Sam couldn't dismiss them. Stress did weird things to people. She just couldn't figure out why they had waited so long to retrieve the item. Bodies took time to decompose. Assuming that it would take longer with the body in the crawlspace under the house, Sam considered another possibility.

More often than not, killers liked to collect trophies from the victims. *Could they have come back for the watch because they wanted something to remember Aaron by?*

Climbing into her Explorer, Sam pushed the thought aside. She didn't want anything to distract her while she was visiting with the family.

Chapter 5

"Come in."

Sam stepped into the home before asking the woman if her husband was at home. In her experience, it was always better to speak with both parents at the same time.

"I'm divorced."

The way she said it made Sam think the split wasn't amicable. Knowing the news had to be delivered, Sam asked if they could sit down.

"Did you find Aaron?"

"We believe so," Sam said, watching the woman for any signs of stress. "Last night, some workers at the community center on Berry Road discovered a body in the house sitting on the back of their property."

The woman nodded her head. "He never ran away, did he?"

"No." Sam gave the woman a few minutes to gather herself before she asked about Aaron's father. While she didn't have any reason to believe that either parent had killed the young man, it was standard procedure to start with the immediate family.

"Aaron's father died when he was four." The woman glanced up at the ceiling for a moment, then made the sign of the cross. "I married Tim right before Aaron started high school. It was a stupid thing to do, but I was struggling to feed us at the time."

"Is that Tim Burwell?" Sam asked, getting ready to write the name down in her notebook.

"Burwell is my first husband's last name. I never changed it after he passed away."

That's interesting, Sam thought.

"Tim's last name is Creighton. Last I heard, he still lives in Novato."

Sam noted the name and address before explaining that they would have to wait for the DNA results to come back before they could declare that they had indeed found Aaron.

"I don't understand. I sent over all of his medical records years ago. Are you saying you're not sure that it's him?"

"The medical examiner is sure," Sam said, feeling like an idiot. "Your son had two screws in his left leg." She waited for the woman to nod her head. "There were also some other prior injuries that the M.E. used in order to confirm Aaron's identity. The DNA is just one of the many procedures we use in a case like this."

"Can you tell me how he died?"

"Right now, we're not sure," Sam said, wanting to spare the woman the nightmare of knowing her only child had been beaten to death, then dumped inside an abandoned house. "I do have a couple of questions, if you don't mind. Can you tell me if Aaron had any enemies? Maybe someone who had threatened him prior to his disappearance."

The woman shook her head. "Everyone loved Aaron. In high school, he was the captain of the football team. If he'd have gotten the chance, I'm sure he'd have gone pro."

Sam didn't look up from her notes. It wasn't her place to tell the woman that less than one percent of high school athletes made the cut. "What about his friends? Can you give me their names?"

"Don't you have all this information? Bill said that he had spoken to everyone who knew Aaron. He's the one who told us that Aaron ran away because we were putting too much pressure on him. Said he couldn't live up to our expectations. But I knew better. Aaron would never…"

"Bill?" Sam asked, cutting the woman off. Although she didn't want to hear it, she knew the question had to be asked.

"Yeah. Bill Edwards. Tim kept insisting that Bill was the best cop on the force and that we were lucky to have him investigating the case."

"Your ex-husband knew Sgt. Edwards?"

"They're related to each other somehow. I never got the full story." The woman stopped speaking. Her eyes were locked on Sam. "Do you think…"

Sam hopped to her feet. She was in uncharted waters

and knew that if she didn't put a stop to the speculation, bad things were going to happen. "Stop right there. I'm not accusing anyone of anything. Camden is still a small town. It's not unusual for us to know the victim."

"You're not telling me something."

It was all that Sam could do to keep from telling the woman the truth. While she didn't believe that Edwards had anything to do with the young man's death, it was inappropriate for him to have worked the case in the first place.

Taking a deep breath, Sam explained that because she was aware of everything that Edwards had done in the case, she couldn't speculate as to why the case had gone unsolved. While it didn't appear to satisfy the woman's curiosity, it did get her to calm down. Then she asked the one question Sam had been dreading. Mrs. Burwell wanted to know when she could see her son.

Sam knew there was nothing she could say to soften the blow, so she went with the truth. Aaron had died twenty-four years ago. All that was left was his bones and a leather wallet.

"I understand." Mrs. Burwell got to her feet, then

asked Sam to leave. She needed time to process the information and figure out what she was going to do next.

Sam was halfway to the door when she remembered what Bobbi had said about someone coming back to retrieve something from the dead body.

"Do you remember if your son wore a watch or any jewelry on his left hand?"

It took a few seconds, then the woman nodded. "His father's watch. He never went anywhere without it."

The instant Sam heard the words, her gut told her that the stepfather had something to do with the boy's disappearance. It all made sense. The guy had to compete against the memory of a dead man. Something no one was capable of doing.

After handing the woman her business card, Sam thanked her for her time, then told her that if she had any questions, she should call the station and ask for her.

"Promise me that you'll catch the person responsible for this."

I'll do better than that. I'll make sure he suffers along with anyone who helped him cover it up, Sam thought. "I'll do my best," she said, opening the front door. As tired as she was, Sam knew she had one more stop to make before she called it a day.

After pulling away from the home, Sam called dispatch to let them know that she was headed up to Santa Rosa to speak with the former police sergeant, Bill Edwards.

Chapter 6

Unable to locate the former police sergeant, Sam swung by the local newspaper office to search through the old newspapers. Luck was on her side. She found one dated July fifth, nineteen ninety-nine. The headline announced Aaron's disappearance. While the details were sketchy, the reporter had managed to speak to the people he had been with the night he had gone missing.

After jotting down the names, Sam moved onto the next one. As Bobbi had remembered, the story had dominated the news for several weeks before the paper decided it was no longer interested in what had happened to the missing teenager.

In the beginning, everyone had an opinion on what

might have happened to the teenager. The theories ranged from a local maniac killing the kid, to him leaving for parts unknown in search of solace. A group of teens from Cotati had sworn they saw him three days after his disappearance, fishing in Spring Lake in Santa Rosa. A girl from Petaluma claimed she had seen him shooting pool on the night he had gone missing.

Only one article mentioned Sgt. Edwards. Two full weeks after Aaron had vanished, the cop told local reporters that the evidence pointed to the teenager leaving town. As far as he was concerned, there was nothing to be worried about.

Leaning back into her chair, Sam wondered why the patrol sergeant hadn't spoken to any of the potential witnesses. While it was possible he had, and just never thought to include it in his report, she knew better. Edwards had always been a lousy cop. A man who had taken the job only because his buddy was the chief. In her opinion, he should have never been given the opportunity to wear the badge.

Shoving the newspapers aside, Sam looked down at her notes. There were more than a dozen people she needed to speak with. Although she knew the odds of them remembering anything were slim, it still had to be done. It was possible they had gotten their dates mixed up and with some gentle prodding might recall a crucial fact overlooked by Edwards.

After putting the newspapers back where she had found them, Sam asked the receptionist if there was anyone on staff who would have been working at the time of the disappearance.

"You know that was twenty-four years ago, right?" the young woman asked.

Sam thanked her anyway. Pointing out that some people made a career out of their job wasn't going to do her any good.

When she got outside, she took one more look at the list of names before calling Jenna. The sergeant had done a little digging of her own and wanted Sam to stop by the station before she called it a day.

Cursing her luck, Sam agreed to come by and check out what her supervisor had found. As she drove out of the parking lot, Sam placed another call to Carol. She needed to speak with her father.

"Is it urgent?" the former prosecutor asked.

Sam rolled her eyes. *What difference does it make why I want to speak with my father?* Instead of voicing her opinion, she informed the woman that she just needed to talk to him about her murder investigation.

"I'll set it up," Carol said.

Hanging up, Sam tossed her phone onto the passenger seat and prayed that Luca would get back soon. The restaurant owner had taken an unexpected vacation and it was making her life miserable. Unlike Carol, the old Italian chef never questioned why Sam wanted something done. He just did it and moved on.

As Sam drove south, she wondered what Jenna had uncovered in her search. Considering the sergeant felt like it was important enough to have her come by the station, Sam believed it had to be tied to Sgt. Edwards in some form or fashion.

The thought brought a smile to her face. In her opinion, the former police sergeant was due for a comeuppance. By being allowed to retire, he had never had to face the consequences of his actions, including his assault on her.

While she knew that she was getting sidetracked, Sam couldn't seem to get the man out of her thoughts. For too many years, he had gotten away with being a bad cop. Not only had it cost the department some good people, but there were also more than a few criminals who had escaped justice because of his actions.

I should have had him put down like a rabid dog, she thought, taking the Expressway exit.

Sam was pulling to a stop at the end of the ramp when she realized that she was thinking like her father. Under normal circumstances, it wouldn't have bothered her, but while she wore the badge, such thoughts were dangerous. They could lead her to make a mistake which would cost all of them their freedom.

While she waited for the light to turn green, Sam turned her attention back to the problem at hand. Someone needed to pay for killing Aaron Burwell. The poor kid had been beaten to death. She found herself wondering what that must have been like for him.

Sam tried to picture the arm bones in her mind. None showed any obvious signs of trauma. That meant he hadn't tried to defend himself from the attack.

Did the first blow kill him? Sam asked herself.

The nagging voice in the back of her mind didn't think so. Whoever had killed Aaron wanted him to suffer. Otherwise, they wouldn't have taken the time to break so many of his ribs.

The sound of a horn blaring pulled Sam from her thoughts. Merging into the left lane, she followed the Expressway until it met up with Stoney Point Road.

"He deserves better," Sam said aloud. In her heart, she knew that she wasn't up to the task. Aaron needed a real detective working on his case. Someone who could uncover twenty-year-old clues and make sure the guilty party got what was coming to them.

Chapter 7

"We're not the only ones who thought Edwards was a bad cop," Jenna said, sliding a sheet of paper across her desk.

Sam grabbed the paper and read the first paragraph wondering why none of the information had been placed in the Burwell file. Skipping ahead, she noted the name at the bottom of the page. Det. Tucker. Her first instinct was to ask Jenna why the guy wasn't sitting in an interrogation room. Then she realized there must be a reason.

"How did you get this?" Sam asked.

"It was emailed to me an hour ago. Tucker heard the story on the news this morning and assumed that we would want to speak with him." Jenna held up a hand to keep Sam from asking the obvious question. "There's a problem."

Sam's eyes dropped back to the email. The last paragraph spelled it all out. After leaving the Camden Police Department, he had taken a job with a private investigation firm in San Francisco. His first case involved a missing child. It turned out that the kid had been taken by members of a human smuggling operation. Detective Dave Tucker was currently in the Witness Protection Program.

"You've got to be kidding me," Sam said, dropping the paper onto the desk. "If he can't talk to us, why bother sending the email?"

Jenna pointed to one of the other passages in the email. "According to Tucker, the house where you found Aaron was once owned by his stepfather's uncle. Who just happens to be Sgt. Edwards' father. A bit of a coincidence if you ask me."

"That's not right," Sam said, pulling her notepad out. "The house was owned by a woman named Kristen Owens. She died like fifteen years ago."

"Kristen Owens was Edwards grandmother. She

gave the house to her son when he got married. Why he never transferred the title over is beyond me, but it doesn't change the fact that Edwards and Aaron's stepfather have a link to the house."

Sam's mind was reeling. Once she proved the pair was linked to the home, the D.A. wouldn't have any other choice but to issue an arrest warrant for the both of them.

"Don't get ahead of yourself," Jenna said. "We still have nothing tying the pair to Aaron's murder. It's possible that someone else killed him and dumped his body in the house to make them look guilty."

"Yeah right." Sam wasn't ready to believe in any conspiracy theory. "Who else could have known the house belonged to their family?"

"Come on," Jenna said. "This town was a lot smaller twenty-five years ago than it is today. Everyone would have known that Edwards grew up in that house."

As much as Sam hated to admit it, Jenna was right. Secrets were still hard to keep in Camden. If she was going to nail Edwards and his cousin, she'd need something linking them to the murder.

"Do you think it's enough to get a search warrant?" Sam asked, thinking about how fun it would be to hand the former police sergeant a search warrant.

"Maybe, but I don't think it's a smart move. Once they find out we're investigating them, any evidence they may have will get destroyed."

"The story broke an hour ago. They have to know that we're going to want to speak with them sooner or later."

"That's not the same as searching their homes. Before we do anything, we need to find all the places where they could have hidden something. A storage unit. A summer cabin. An old clunker sitting on a farm somewhere. I don't want to give these guys a chance to destroy the evidence just because we were in a hurry to arrest them."

Sam was amazed at how well her supervisor's mind worked. If the shoe had been on the other foot, she'd have already sent someone to pick up Edwards and Creighton.

"Have you replied to Detective Tucker's email?"

"I suspect he created the account right before he sent

it. If he's telling the truth, he won't risk checking the account to see whether or not I replied."

"You haven't checked out his story yet?" Sam couldn't believe it. Jenna was a lot of things, but stupid wasn't among them.

"I made some 'unofficial' phone calls to make sure that he wasn't retired and living in Florida. Based on what I was told, this is on the up and up. Plus, I can verify everything else in the email."

"Maybe I should have Gary look into it. Just to make sure the guy is on the level."

"If you ask him about someone in the Witness Protection Program, he's going to want to know why you're asking. That could cause a lot of problems for us and Detective Tucker."

"You're right," Sam conceded, knowing that she had other ways to find out if in fact the former detective was in the program or not. One phone call to Carol would do the trick. "So how do you want to proceed?"

"I want you to talk to everyone who knew Aaron. See if we can't place him with Edwards or his stepfather on the day he went missing. In the meantime, I'll have

Amy and James pull up everything we can find on the pair. Including any property their family might own in the area."

"Okay." Sam stretched as she got up. "I'm going to head home and get a few hours of sleep. I'll see you this afternoon."

Chapter 8

Sam woke to the smell of burnt bacon. Rolling over, she checked the clock next to her bed. It had been less than four hours since she had laid down. Cursing herself for allowing her cousin to install her alarm system, Sam got out of bed and grabbed the t-shirt lying on top of the clothes hamper. Although it had seen better days, she wasn't concerned about making a good impression. She just wanted a few more hours of sleep.

"Why are you in my house?"

Chris ignored her question as he took another bite of eggs. "Why are you sleeping in the middle of the day? I thought you were still working the day shift."

Hitting the brew button on the coffee machine, Sam

explained that she had caught a murder case the night before and hadn't gotten any sleep since.

"The one on the news?" Chris picked up his plate and took it over to the sink. "Is there anything we can do to help?"

While Sam appreciated the offer, she didn't want her cousins anywhere near the case. It had been less than two weeks since the kidnapping charges had been dismissed against them and she didn't want to give the acting D.A. any reason to regret her decision.

"No thanks." Sam took a sip of the coffee, then carried it over to the table. "Have you spoken to my dad lately?"

"I saw him last night."

"Did he happen to mention why Luca left town?" In Sam's mind, there could be only one reason as to why the old Italian had dropped everything to return to Italy. Someone was in trouble.

"His mother is dying." Chris shook his head in amazement. "I thought for sure the old hag was going to outlive all of us. Remember the time she whipped me and Paul with that ketchup bottle?"

"You were trying to run her dog over," Sam said, replaying the scene in her mind.

The boys must have been in their early teens at the time. For reasons neither would explain, they had gotten the idea in their heads that it would be fun to chase the old woman's dog around with their bicycles. Despite her advanced age, she had caught the teens before they could succeed in their mission.

"That was still no excuse to hit us with a glass bottle. She's lucky she didn't kill us."

As the memory faded, Sam remembered that her cousin hadn't answered her question. "You still haven't told me why you're here."

"I need a favor," he said, rummaging through her refrigerator. "Why don't you ever have anything for dessert?"

"To start with, I'm never home. Besides, when I want something for dessert, I go to L'ultima cena and let Luca make it for me."

"You could still keep ice cream or maybe some donuts around in case someone stops by. It never hurts to be a good host."

Sam had reached her breaking point. She demanded that he get out of her refrigerator and tell her why he had stopped by.

"We've been through this," he said, opening the cabinets. "Don't you ever go shopping? I've seen homeless people who have more groceries than you do."

"I swear to God, if you don't tell me what you want, I'm going to go get my gun and shoot you."

Chris paused to look over and roll his eyes. "Like I said, I need you to do me a favor." He stopped speaking long enough to pull a box of crackers from the cabinet. Leaving the door open, he returned to the table and took a seat across from her. "I need you to speak to the mayor for me."

For a brief moment, Sam could have sworn she felt the earth come to a grinding halt. While she could come up with dozens of reasons as to why her cousin would take an interest in the mayor, she knew that she didn't want any part of the scheme he had in his mind.

"Before you say no, let me tell you why you need to speak with him." Chris took one bite of the cracker before getting up and tossing the rest in the trash. "These things are stale."

"Why do you need me to talk to the mayor?"

"Remember that gambling ring your D.A. was running? The mayor had a piece of the action."

Sam didn't want to think about how her cousin knew the mayor was involved. "What does this have to do with me?"

"The mayor is thinking about starting the game up again. I want you to go by and let him know that's a bad idea."

"And how do you suggest that I do that?" Sam asked. If she were honest with her cousin, she'd rather stick her tongue in the blender than to tell the mayor that she knew he was getting ready to start up an illegal gambling ring.

"I don't care how you do it, just do it. If this guy starts the game up again, I'm going to bury him and his family in the quarry."

Sam knew her cousin wasn't joking. He rarely joked when it came to murdering someone, and the fact that he named a specific location told her that he had put some thought into what would happen if she failed to do as he asked.

"How much time do I have?"

"He wants to have the game up and running before Labor Day. From what I heard, some big wigs are coming down from Sacramento and he wants to show them that he has what it takes to run the operation."

"Can't you talk to him yourself? I'm sure that if you explained what the consequences are, he'd have a change of heart."

"I don't want him to know that we bugged his house."

Sam felt sick. She remembered something about him remodeling the mayor's house but had never considered the thought of him bugging the place.

I should have known.

Weighing the options, Sam felt as if she didn't have a choice. The city had already lost two city councilmen over the gambling ring. If the mayor and his family suddenly vanished, it would have a ripple effect on everyone who called Camden home.

"I'll figure out something," she said, wondering how long it would take her to come up with a plan. "If I need it, can you give me the names of some of the other people?"

"I'd rather not involve anyone else."

Sam knew what that meant. Her family had plans for the other parties involved. At some point, they'd either blackmail them with the information, or kill them.

"Fine. Give me a few days to work on this murder case, then I'll go see the mayor."

"I knew that I could count on you." Chris reached into his pocket and pulled out a thick envelope. "Your father asked me to give this to you."

Chapter 9

Sam didn't bother to count the cash inside the envelope. She already had more money than she could spend in one lifetime. It was the frequency in which the envelopes were delivered that troubled her. Over the past few weeks, Sam had gotten three payments. Payments which she was sure were intended to help her make the decision she had been avoiding.

Shoving the cash into the safe, Sam closed the lid, then leaned up against the wall. Her father wasn't making the decision any easier. While he hadn't come out and said it, she could tell that he wanted her to give up her life as Sam Wright and take her rightful place among the family.

While the thought was tantalizing, Sam wasn't ready to give up on her life. She enjoyed being a cop. Day after day, she got to help people who were unable to help themselves. That would stop if she became a mobster. The family was only concerned about themselves. Shaking the thought from her mind, Sam walked into the bathroom and took a shower.

After calling Jenna to let her know that she was heading out to speak with the first witness, Sam made a mental note to talk to Carol about what her life would be like should she choose to take a leadership role in the family business.

Sam was getting into her Explorer when she saw her neighbor from across the street headed in her direction. Like always, Christine seemed to be in crisis mode.

"I'm so glad I caught you," the retired nurse said, wiping the sweat off her brow. "Have you heard the news? They found that Burwell boy last night."

"Did you know him?" Sam asked.

"I knew him better than most. He dated my daughter all through high school."

Hopping out of the SUV, Sam suggested they go inside and talk about Aaron Burwell.

"What do you want to know?" Christine asked, wrapping her hands around the coffee mug.

"How did Aaron and your daughter meet?" Sam asked, trying to picture the two of them as a couple. From what little she knew about the pair; they seemed like polar opposites.

"They met back in middle school, but it wasn't until the summer before high school that things went in a different direction. Anyway, that summer, something changed in Aaron. He went from this shy boy who never talked to anyone to this outgoing stud, bent on spreading his seed all over town. I never saw anything like it before."

Although Sam had a hundred questions she wanted to ask, she had learned to never interrupt a witness unless it was necessary.

"Once he met Megan, he changed again. All of a sudden, he got interested in sports, and boy could he play. Made the first string in his freshman year. Most of us knew he'd go pro after he got out of school, but then he had his accident, and everything changed."

"Back up," Sam said, hoping she could get the woman back on track. "Tell me about that first summer he and your daughter dated."

For the next half an hour, Christine recalled everything she could remember about the relationship Aaron had with her daughter, including catching the pair exploring their bodies.

"What kind of kid was he?" Sam asked. "Do you remember him getting into any trouble?"

"Only with that stepfather of his. Tim something. Oh, that man used to drink something awful. It seemed like every other week he'd end up in a fight or in jail because of it. If it hadn't been for that cousin of his, they'd have locked him up long ago."

Not wanting to put ideas in the woman's head, Sam didn't mention Sgt. Edwards name. Instead she asked Christine if she could remember who it was that kept Tim out of jail.

"It was the chief. Roy Carpenter was a good old boy if there ever was one. As long as you stayed on his good side, you could get away with murder in this town. The rumor was, he had one of his guys in the department run Aaron over because he had lost a big game against Santa Rosa."

"Are you saying the chief had a teenager run over because of a football game?" Sam asked, wondering if it was possible the old chief had been involved in the murder. From what little she knew about the man; it wouldn't surprise her.

"I'm not saying it's true, but it was the talk of the town for weeks. Do you know Jackie Solomon? She worked over at the salon on fourth street back then. She told me the chief had lost more than five grand on that game."

Sam knew Jackie well. Even though the woman was well into her eighties, she still kept her ear to the ground. If anything tawdry was happening within the city limits, she was sure to know about it. The best part was her mind was still as sharp as it ever was.

"After the accident, Aaron was never the same. He broke up with Megan and swore he'd never play football again. As you can imagine, that upset quite a few people around here. Aaron was their meal ticket. When he suited up, you couldn't lose."

"What do you mean?" Sam asked, feeling like she was on the verge of a great discovery.

"In the three and a half years he spent playing football, he only lost one game. I can still remember the night they lost to Santa Rosa. It should have been a blowout, but for whatever reason, Aaron threw two interceptions that night. The second one cost them the game."

Sam glanced at her watch. If she wanted to find out why Aaron had lost that game, she needed to get a move on.

"Thanks," she said, getting out of her chair. "I gotta go, but I'd like to talk to you more about this later."

"Anytime."

Chapter 10

Jail had not smoothed the rough edges off of Megan's personality. The moment Sam sat down across from her in the visiting room, the woman launched into a tirade, where she accused the detective of everything from framing her, to committing unnatural acts with half the farm animals in the state.

"Is that the mouth you kiss your mother with?" Sam asked, growing more tired of the woman with each passing second.

"You're the one who asked for this meeting," the public defender stated. "My client is just expressing her opinion. She doesn't mean anything by it."

"Yes I do," Megan shouted. "This pig framed me."

Sam got to her feet and started for the door. "I'm sorry that I wasted your time," she said to the attorney.

"Hold on a second." The public defender leaned over and whispered something to Megan. Whatever it was, seemed to have an effect on the woman, because she calmed down immediately. Then the lawyer turned back to Sam and let her know that if her client cooperated, she wanted the detective to speak to the acting D.A. on her behalf.

"It depends on whether or not she has anything useful to say."

Megan flashed Sam a smile that revealed several missing teeth. "I know everything. And if you want my help putting the person away, I want a walk."

"Not going to happen," Sam said, not caring that the woman had less than six months left on her sentence. As far as she was concerned, the woman could rot.

"Then why did you come here?"

"I thought you might want to do the right thing for the first time in your life." Sam watched the woman for any sign that she still cared about Aaron. "If you cooperate, I could make sure that you get your phone privileges back."

"How'd you know that my client's phone privileges had been revoked?" the attorney asked. "Have you been keeping tabs on her?"

"As a matter of fact, I have," Sam said. "On top of assaulting me, your client has taken it upon herself to harass her mother twenty-four hours a day."

"I've never…" Megan fell silent when her lawyer placed a hand on her arm.

"If you want my client's cooperation in this murder investigation, you're going to have to offer her something more than restoring phone privileges."

"Okay." Sam reached up and tapped her chin as if she were considering what else she might offer the woman. "If what your client has to say leads to an arrest and conviction, I'll see that a hundred dollars gets put into her account."

"You're going to have to do better than that, Detective. From what I've heard, you have no idea who committed this murder or why they did it."

"I've got an idea," Sam said, walking back over to

the table. "If your client refuses to tell me what she knows, when I get back to Camden, I'll call up every reporter in the bay area and tell them that we have a cooperating witness, who's willing to name names in exchange for an early release from prison. It shouldn't take the murderer long to put two and two together."

"Is that a threat, Detective?"

Sam nodded her head. She was done playing games with the both of them. Megan was either going to talk or she wasn't, and at that point, she no longer cared. It wasn't like the woman had any concrete proof linking the murderer to the crime. At best, she might know who it was.

"Can she do that?" Megan asked.

"I can, and I will," Sam responded. "Let me be honest with you. I don't give a crap what happens to you in here. If I'm right about who killed Aaron, they have friends in this place."

The look that passed across Megan's face told Sam that she was wrong about who killed Aaron. The convict turned to her lawyer and told her that she no longer felt like talking to the detective.

"Looks like we're done here," the lawyer said, getting out of the chair. "Your bluff didn't work. Let me know if you're serious about learning the truth, but I can tell you now, it's going to cost you. My client expects to walk in exchange for her information, and I'm going to make sure everyone knows you're the reason the murderer is still walking around free as a bird."

Crap. Sam remained silent as she exited the room. The thought that the murderer was someone other than the stepfather or one of his relatives on the police force had never crossed her mind. Thinking back to what Christine had said about Aaron being a sure thing when he suited up, Sam realized that she shouldn't have been so quick to leap to the obvious conclusion. Everyone who had bet on the teenager had a reason to want him dead.

As Sam stood in the hallway, she called Marsha Dillon. The acting district attorney wasn't surprised that Megan wanted a deal in writing before she talked.

"What do you think?" Marsha asked. "Does she know who killed him?"

"It's possible," Sam admitted. She wasn't ready to

tell Marsha that her theory was wrong. "We have another problem. Her lawyer is threatening to go to the press if we don't give Megan a deal."

"They all say that. I can ask the judge for a gag order if you think it's necessary. That should buy us a little more time to figure out what she knows."

"What if we go to the press?" Sam asked, thinking it would be nice to put the shoe on the other foot. In her mind, she believed the woman would fold in a heartbeat if the public knew she was protecting a murderer.

"Let me think about it. In the meantime, see what you can find out."

Chapter 11

Sam looked around to make sure that no one was nearby, then she called Carol. The bar owner greeted her by letting her know that her father was back in town.

"Is he in Windsor or the city?" Sam asked, hoping the former assistant prosecutor would tell her that Tony was in the north bay.

"He's in the city." There was a short pause before Carol asked Sam how the case was going.

Sam gave her as many details as she could, then laid out the theory she had been working on. As the words tumbled out of her mouth, she could see why she had leaped to the obvious conclusion that the former police chief or sergeant had been involved. It all made perfect sense.

"So what's the problem?" Carol asked.

"When I mentioned it to the witness, the woman almost laughed at me. Somehow, I got on the wrong track." Sam shook her head in disgust. "What do you think?"

"From what you've told me, it sounds like everyone in town had a reason to want this kid dead. He was their meal ticket."

"I was thinking the same thing, but it doesn't make sense. Why kill the only guy who can make you rich?" Then the reason became clear. "He didn't want to play football anymore."

"Sounds like a good motive to me," Carol said. "It's possible someone tried to convince the kid to change his mind and things got out of hand."

Sam had begun to consider that possibility. It would also explain why someone had hit Aaron with a car earlier in the year. Thinking back, Sam remembered her father resorting to the same method when someone didn't want to cooperate. First, a message was sent. A broken arm or leg, then if they still didn't listen something worse would happen to them.

"Call dad and let him know that I'll be coming by as soon as I get the chance. I want to run something by him." Sam was about to say goodbye when another thought hit her. "What do you think about me going to the press to let them know our witness won't cooperate without a deal?"

"What do they want?"

"She wants a get out of jail free card."

"I'm guessing you don't want that to happen." Carol let out an audible sigh. "Sometimes you have to look at the big picture. Can this witness tell you who did it? If so, you might have to suck it up and give them what they want."

"I know that deals get made every day, but this is the woman who tried to assault me a while back. I'd rather not put her back on the street unless I have to."

"Would you like your father to send someone to talk to her?"

"No," Sam said a little too quickly. "If she gets the snot beat out of her right after I paid her a visit, everyone's going to point the finger at me. I can't afford that kind of scrutiny right now."

"Then let me bring that profiler in. The one I told you about."

"No way. Don't you remember what happened the last time we brought the feds in?"

"This is different. Lisa specializes in cold cases. It's like some sort of calling or something."

Sam didn't want to hear it. She already had one federal agent in her life. Adding another would be like pouring salt on the wound. "Thanks anyway, but I think I'll pass."

"Let me know if you change your mind."

"I will," Sam said, preparing to hang up. Then she remembered that Carol hadn't answered her question about going to the press, so she asked a second time.

"If it's played right, it could get you the information you want, but it could also blow up in your face. We used to do that kind of thing all the time back in Jersey. Then we ended up getting one of our witnesses killed and the D.A. put a stop to it. I'll say this. If you're thinking of going that route, get everyone on board first. That way no one can throw you under the bus should things go south."

"Thanks," Sam said. "I'll let you know what we decide to do."

Hanging up, Sam glanced over at the visitor's room. While she had no desire to go back inside and speak with Megan again, she knew it was necessary.

"What'd they say?" the lawyer asked, as Sam entered the room. "Are they going to offer my client a deal in exchange for what she knows?"

"It doesn't sound like it," Sam said, keeping the frustration out of her voice. She turned and looked at Megan. "I wouldn't get my hopes up if I were you."

"We'll see about that," Megan replied, before whispering something to her attorney.

Sam had the feeling that the rug was about to be pulled out from underneath her. Knowing it would be better to get out of there before she did something stupid, Sam exited the room. When she reached the end of the hall, she let the guard know she was done with the prisoner and that he could take her back to her cell at his convenience.

At the sign in desk, Sam asked the young man behind the counter if anyone had come to visit Megan since she had arrived at the prison.

After typing her name into the computer, he shook his head. "Just you and her public defender."

Chapter 12

With everyone gathered in the briefing room, Sam shared her initial feelings on the case, then proceeded to let them know how her meeting with Megan Johnson had gone. As expected, Jenna and Lieutenant Cox were reluctant to release a statement to the press. They argued that it had too much potential to backfire.

"What if we make it look like her attorney was the one who reached out to the media?" Amy asked. "Think about it. We have someone we know claim a witness knows something about the murder and the cops aren't willing to make a deal for the information. When they call to get our side of the story, we neither confirm nor deny the statement."

Sam was shocked. Amy was the least devious person she knew. Yet somehow, the demure detective had come up with the perfect plan.

"It could still blow up in our faces," Lt. Cox said. "If anyone finds out we were behind the leak, we could face criminal charges for endangering Mrs. Johnson's life."

"It was their idea to go to the press." Amy glanced over at Sam. "Isn't that what they told you?"

"That's neither here nor there," the lieutenant said. "Lawyers threaten to go to the media all the time. I'm not about to put their lives in danger just because we can." He turned to Sam. "Is there any proof this woman is telling the truth?"

"I'm not sure. What I do know, is that she doesn't think that Edwards or the old chief had anything to do with it. When I floated the idea that the murderer had a friend who might be working at the prison, she all but laughed in my face."

"Okay. So if neither of them were involved, where does that leave us?"

"I think we should eliminate the old chief. And

while it's still possible that Edwards helped cover it up, I'm thinking he just did the least amount of work possible because he wanted to forget about Aaron and move onto something else." Sam walked over to the white board and drew a big question mark beside the step father's name.

"Are you ready to eliminate him also?" the lieutenant asked.

"Not yet. From what my neighbor told me, they were fighting on a regular basis. Plus, there's the whole name thing. When Mrs. Burwell married him, she refused to take his name or allow Aaron to change his. I could see how that could eat at a guy."

"Tell us more about your betting theory," Jenna said. "How does that play into all of this?"

For the next half hour, Sam explained how a large segment of the town's population made money betting on the games. That led her to the theory that someone had tried to teach Aaron a lesson after he threw the game against Santa Rosa.

When Sam pulled up the hit and run case, she indicated that Sgt. Edwards had also been in charge of the investigation, and then showed how it had been mishandled from the beginning.

The lieutenant pointed out that it wasn't unusual to be assigned cases involving friends and family. While not ideal, things like that happened in a small town where everyone knew each other.

"I get that," Sam said, knowing he was right. "But we're talking about putting the least qualified person on the case. Twice."

"Maybe they were busy at the time," Lt. Cox offered. "You know what it's like when we have our hands full. Things fall through the cracks."

"Tucker thought something was wrong," Sam said, trying to put the conversation back on track. "It's why he reached out when he heard Aaron's body was discovered."

Jenna filled the lieutenant in on the email from the former detective and her efforts to prove its authenticity. She added that in her opinion, they should operate on the idea that the letter was, in fact, genuine.

"It's still hearsay." Lt. Cox drummed his fingers on the table as he looked over the white board. "For now, let's stick with what we know. The house belonged to Sgt. Edward's family. He is related to Aaron's stepfather. And he was the chief investigator in two crimes committed against our victim." He looked around the room. "Anything else?"

"He did the least amount of work possible," Amy added. "I've looked at both files. Between the two of them, he talked to less than ten people. It was like he didn't want to know who attacked Aaron."

"Or he knew who did it and didn't want anyone else finding out," Sam said. "Maybe Edwards was in on the fix. And when things went sideways, he made sure no one found out about it."

"What fix?" Jenna asked.

Sam walked over to the second white board and wrote the word "Bookie" at the top. "Someone set the odds, took the bets, collected the money and paid out the winners. They also had to control the outcome of the game somehow."

"If they were dictating the outcome, how did Aaron manage to lose the game?"

"He threw a crucial interception which cost them the

win." Sam turned to the board and wrote the word "lesson" underneath the hit and run case. Then she explained how it fit into her narrative.

The lieutenant got up and walked over to the first board. "Let me see if I have this straight. Someone figured out a way to rig the football games. Things are going along well until one day, Aaron gets it in his head that he no longer wants to play along, so they teach him a lesson by hitting him with a car. That sparks him to give up the game, which in turn, causes someone to kill him."

"I don't think they meant to kill him," Sam said, pointing at the timeline she had drawn on the first board. "From what my neighbor told me, Aaron didn't make the decision to skip college until after he graduated. That's when they decided to teach him another lesson."

"I'm not buying it," the lieutenant said. "Even if you're right about everything else, there's no way they could have fixed the college games."

That thought had not crossed Sam's mind. Turning to the board, she tried to come up with another explanation for why the murderer had killed Aaron. If it wasn't about the money, she'd have to start over from scratch.

Failing to come up with another reason, Sam walked back over to the table and took a seat next to Amy. She couldn't believe that once again she had fallen for the obvious trap. Looking at the others, she wondered if they were losing faith in her. If they were, she didn't blame them. Without her family backing her up, she was lost.

Jenna got up and added a new line to the board. "Why would someone want Aaron dead?"

Chapter 13

Within minutes, they had come up with a list of possible motives, but nothing that helped them narrow down the list of possible suspects. Amy believed it boiled down to jealousy or revenge. Both were powerful feelings that often led to murder.

Sam still felt that money played some kind of role in the decision. In her mind, she could picture someone thinking they could get rich once Aaron was selected by the right college. Although college athletes were forbidden from profiting from their given sports, it didn't stop alumni from funneling cash to their families.

Soon, Amy was able to win over the lieutenant and Jenna. The pair agreed that the detective was on the right track and insisted that Sam keep that in mind while she conducted the investigation.

Taking the lead, Amy wiped the white boards clean, then wrote "motives" at the top of the first one. After the list was complete, she asked the group who benefited from Aaron's death.

"We know he was a star athlete," Jenna said. "That had to ruffle some feathers. Do we know who the backup quarterback was?"

Sam looked at the file. "As far as I can tell, Edwards never spoke with his teammates or coach." Playing off Amy's idea, she made a note to check out the other players on the team. "We also need to find out who was rigging the games."

"That's a good idea." Jenna turned to Amy. "I want you to talk to anyone you can find who played with Aaron. See if any of them had a reason to want him dead. We also need to find out if any of them knew the games were being rigged."

As Amy wrote down her assignments, Jenna turned to Sam and told her to follow the money. If Aaron was killed because he had cost the wrong person money, she wanted to know who had lost the most.

It was after three o'clock when the lieutenant suggested they call it a day. Like it or not, there were still plenty of other cases that needed to be solved. A twenty-five-year-old murder wasn't, in his opinion, the most important thing they had on their plates.

Although Sam didn't agree with her boss, she wasn't about to argue with him about it. Aaron Burwell wasn't going anywhere. Besides, it would be weeks before they got the lab results, and she still needed to speak with the mayor about his gambling problem.

After agreeing to keep everyone up to date on the investigation, Sam packed up her belongings and headed for the door. She made it ten feet when her phone started to ring. Seeing the district attorney's number, she turned around and held up a hand to keep everyone from leaving.

"Go ahead Marsha, I've got you on speaker."

"You're not going to believe this," the acting D.A. said. "Megan's lawyer held a press conference after she left the prison. She's claiming that my office and your department are conspiring to protect the murderer. She's asking that the feds take over the case."

"Let me call you right back." Sam looked over at the lieutenant. "What do you want to do?"

He suggested they wait there while he talked to the chief about it. Sam wasn't surprised that he didn't want to be the one who made the decision. If they did the wrong thing, heads were going to roll. As tempted as she was to reach out to her family, Sam knew that wasn't the answer. At best, they'd only make things worse.

While she had no doubt that they'd be able to get the answers she needed, she didn't want to deal with the aftermath. There were only two options left once they got the information out of someone. They'd either frame them or make them disappear. In Megan's case, framing her wouldn't prevent her from talking. That meant the woman would have to die, and Sam wasn't willing to kill her friend's daughter.

When the lieutenant returned, he told them that any decision made would have to come from the district attorney's office. As far as the Camden Police Department was concerned, they took no position on any deal made between the prosecutor and the prisoner.

"It's all about the politics," Sam said, instantly regretting it. She knew it wasn't the lieutenant's fault. No matter what choice the department made, someone would say it was wrong. "Forget I said anything."

"I don't like it either, but the city hasn't approved our annual budget yet and the chief doesn't want to do anything that could cause them to slash it again."

Sam wondered what the world would be like if the police were allowed to do their jobs. While she understood that some departments might take things to the extreme in order to prevent crime, she still believed that overall, life would be better.

"You heard the man," Jenna said, pushing her way past Sam and Amy. "No comment whenever possible. If they don't like it, tell them to call the public information officer."

Grabbing her purse, Sam gave the sergeant and lieutenant a quick half-hearted salute before she exited the room.

Just because their hands are tied doesn't mean mine are, she thought.

The plan was simple. Once she was out of the building, she'd call Carol and have things set right. Right or wrong, she wasn't about to let some prisoner blackmail her department into letting her go.

There's more than one way to skin a cat, Sam said to herself. She just needed them to reach out to their people in the media. No violence. No threats. Just get the truth out to everyone living in the bay area. *What could go wrong?*

Chapter 14

Sam was about to call Carol when another thought popped into her mind. If she ended up getting Megan killed by leaking her name to the press, she'd never be able to live with herself. Good or bad, Megan was Christine's daughter and Sam hated to cause the retired nurse any pain.

Thinking it would be better to do nothing, Sam got into her unmarked Ford and drove over to city hall. While she wasn't able to do anything about Megan, she could save the mayor's life. All she had to do was convince the man to give up on his plans to restart the illegal gambling operation.

It had been a while since Sam had visited city hall.

The last time she had walked through the doors, she had been treated like a hero. Her investigation had proven to everyone that no one was above the law. As she parked in the visitor's lot, Sam wondered if she'd get the same treatment after she told the mayor she knew about his plans to pick up where the two convicted city councilmen had left off.

"Good afternoon, Detective," the secretary said, as Sam approached her desk. "Do you have an appointment?"

"I don't," Sam answered, keeping her voice low. "I just need a few minutes of the mayor's time to discuss a personal matter."

"Are the city planners still giving you a hard time about the dog park?"

Sam had to smile. After the homeowner's association voted to allow a dog park to be built in her neighborhood, some of the residents turned to the city to get the project terminated. Their efforts had failed, but they weren't ready to give up. The most vocal members had gone to the mayor.

When Sam failed to answer, the secretary gave her

a wink, then picked up the phone. A few seconds later, she told Sam to go on in.

"Thanks," Sam said, turning toward the office.

Although she had been given permission to enter the room, Sam stopped to knock on the door before opening it. A second later, she heard the mayor mumble something to the effect of "come in."

"Good afternoon," she said, pushing the door closed. "I hate to bother you at the office, but this couldn't wait."

Like all politicians, he tried hard to keep the interest off his face, but Sam could tell he was intrigued by her presence. After offering her a drink, he invited her to sit down.

Not wanting to spook the man, Sam explained that while no one had said anything specific, there were rumors of his name being mentioned in conjunction with the ongoing investigation regarding the illegal gambling ring.

"I don't understand," he said, fumbling with his tie. "I thought that case was over. Didn't they all plead guilty?"

"They did." Sam paused to look over her shoulder. She wanted to make him think that she was on his side. "As you may have heard, I've been dating a federal agent who's in charge of the organized crime unit. In passing, he mentioned that some people are trying to link you to the games."

The mayor hopped out of his chair and began straightening his jacket. He looked like a man who was ready to make a break for it. Sam knew that if she didn't calm him down, things were going to get ugly fast.

"Everyone knows you weren't involved," she said, hoping that would do the trick. "We just thought you should know that people are talking. Gary, that's my boyfriend, he thinks it's coming from someone who wants your job, but you never know. It could just be someone who's unhappy with some decision you've made."

"People are always unhappy about something," he said, reaching back for his chair. Although he had begun to sweat, he seemed to be feeling more confident about the situation. "Should I be worried about this?"

"Like I said, the feds know you weren't involved,

but if these rumors persist, they may have to conduct a formal investigation just to satisfy the people who are making these claims."

"But I haven't done anything wrong."

Sam had to bite her lip to keep from calling the man a liar. He had the worst "tell" of anyone she knew. It made her wonder how he had ever managed to get elected. After taking a deep breath, she explained that as long as he paid attention to where he went and who he hung out with, there wouldn't be any problems.

When they were done talking, the mayor walked Sam to the door. Before she could open it, he told her how much he appreciated the heads up. Then he flashed her a huge smile and let her know that he owed her one.

You have no idea, Sam thought.

"By the way," he said, as the door swung open. "I heard you're working the Aaron Burwell case. How's that going?"

"Right now, the only thing that I can tell you is that we know he never left town." Sam started to turn away when she noticed the mayor wasn't surprised to hear the news. "Were you living in Camden when he went missing?"

"Yeah, I was. He dated the girl who lived next door to me for a while. Jamie something. As a matter of fact, I think they were together on the night he went missing. I remember it because when I woke up the next morning, the cops had our street blocked off."

"That must have made things interesting."

"It did." The mayor took a step back, then remembered to smile again. "Well, I don't want to keep you. I know you must be busy." He leaned close. "And thanks again for the heads up."

Chapter 15

Sam didn't waste any time driving over to the Last Call. Although she didn't believe the mayor had anything to do with Aaron's murder, it was clear that he knew something about it, and she wanted to find out what it was. Given the fact that he had been interested in starting up another gambling operation, Sam knew her family would have done a thorough background check on the man.

Parking in the back lot, Sam slipped through the backdoor and went straight to Carol's office. As usual, the bar owner was watching the video monitors, looking for the family's next potential victim.

"What's up?" she asked, turning away from the

video screens. She motioned for Sam to have a seat. "I didn't expect to see you today. Are you on your way to see your father?"

Ignoring the question, Sam asked Carol if she had anything on the mayor that might tie him to the murder.

"I gave everything to Chris," she said. "He'd have mentioned something if there was."

Sam knew the woman was right. Anything out of the ordinary would have been flagged for further study. If the man had been implicated in any way, her family would have already figured out a way to use it to their advantage. Blackmail was one of their biggest money makers.

"You think he might be the killer?"

"I don't think so, but he knows something," Sam said, remembering how freaked out he got when she mentioned that they knew Aaron had never left town. "The guy's like the worst poker player in the world."

"Speaking of poker. Did you convince him to stay out of the gambling business?"

"I told him that the feds had heard his name mentioned a few times." Sam glanced over at the wall of monitors. Doing a quick count in her mind, she estimated there were about twenty cops in the building. "How are things here?"

"Same old, same old. Your friend Susan was in here last night. She was getting all buddy-buddy with that A.D.A. who can't keep her mouth shut."

Isn't that great? Sam thought. She couldn't imagine why someone like Susan would get involved with Sally, but things had changed since Susan's husband had been arrested.

"Just so you know. Your friend was trying to work out a deal to keep her husband off of death row."

"California doesn't kill anybody."

"No, but they do have a habit of passing out life sentences like they're candy." Carol reached into the desk and pulled out a thumb drive. "Want to hear their conversation?"

Sam waved her off. Whatever Susan was up to, was none of her business. She just wished her family felt the same way. From what she had heard, the defense attorney had given up her quest to prove that the mafia was behind every major crime in the county, so they no longer had a reason to keep tabs on her.

Putting the device back in the drawer, Carol turned her attention back to the monitors. "See that guy in the blue shirt playing pool? He's the one who shot that guy over in Sebastopol last week."

"It was a good shooting," Sam said without thinking. "The guy had a hammer in his hand. There was nothing else he could do."

"I'm not saying he did anything wrong."

"Then why point him out?" Sam asked. Then she realized there could be only one reason. The man had been talking about the shooting or something related to it. "Please don't ruin his life."

"Why do you always assume that we're looking to take advantage of people?" Carol rolled her eyes, then used a remote to zoom in on the guy. "That's the fifth beer he's had since he came in. If someone doesn't get him the help he needs, he's either going to kill himself or someone else. The guy's a walking timebomb."

Sam watched the man as he took another sip of his beer. No matter what she did, she couldn't imagine what he was going through. Clean shooting or not, it had to be eating the guy up inside. It was the one thing that the public always got wrong when it came to an officer involved shooting. No cop ever wanted to shoot someone. Taking a life was something you never forgot.

"Do you know what kind of car he's driving?"

Carol rolled her eyes again, then pointed to the monitor that showed the main parking lot. "The black sedan is his. I've already had someone flatten the two back tires."

Excusing herself, Sam stepped out of the office and called Amy. After letting her know that the guy was on a bender, she suggested that the detective reach out to one of her friends in the Sheriff's Department to let them know that one of their own was on a collision course with death.

"I'll take care of it," Amy said. "Just make sure he doesn't leave the bar before the cavalry arrives. Do whatever it takes."

"We're already on it," Sam replied, thinking that even if the man wanted to leave, there was no way he was doing it behind the wheel of his car. "Just don't take too long, okay?"

After she got off the phone, Sam made her way into the main area of the bar and spoke with two of the Santa Rosa cops she knew. Both officers had been keeping an eye on the guy without being obvious about it. While they didn't want to jam the man up, they weren't about to let him get himself into trouble if it were at all possible.

"Thanks," Sam said, shaking both of their hands. "It shouldn't be long before his buddies get here."

With that settled, Sam made her way over to the bar and asked the bartender to cut the deputy off. If all went well, his friends would arrive before he finished his current beer.

"I wouldn't count on it," the bartender said. "The guy's been putting them down as fast as I can fill them up."

"Then give him a non-alcoholic beer." The bartender looked at her as if she had lost her mind. "Fine. The least you could do is water it down before you give it to him."

"You're kidding, right?"

Sam shot the man a look that told him she wasn't

kidding. "We only need to buy a half hour at most. Do what you have to do to keep that man from drinking another beer."

The bartender looked past Sam to the man attempting to shoot pool, then nodded. "I'll do it, but if he starts giving me any lip, you better come over and do something about it."

At first, Sam thought the large man was joking, then she realized that Carol would have him killed if he ever said something stupid to one of her customers. Short of pulling out a gun and shooting everyone in the place, the cops who entered the Last Call were allowed to do whatever they wanted.

"Don't worry, he won't say a word."

Chapter 16

Watching the off-duty deputy fill the car's tire with air, Sam was grateful that Carol had gone above and beyond to make sure the situation had not gone from bad to worse. At the end of the day, she may have saved the guy's life by making sure he couldn't drive the car.

"I hope he gets the help that he needs," Carol said, turning away from the monitor. "It's not going to be easy."

Sam nodded as she sent a text to Amy, thanking her for her assistance in the matter. "They'll make sure he talks to someone. You did good," she added. "Sometimes I forget that you have a soft spot in your heart for cops."

"Some of my best friends are cops."

Seeing that as an opportunity to ask about what it was like to work for the family, Sam asked Carol how she handled being tied to the mafia.

"It's not hard at all," Carol said, closing her eyes. "When I was ten years old, our neighbor's dog bit my little brother. My dad did the right thing and called the police. You can imagine how well that went over with our neighbor."

The woman's story was all too familiar. When Sam had been a patrol officer, one of the most common complaints they received came from feuding neighbors. More often than not, a minor problem would escalate into a full-blown war, all because the police were powerless to put a stop to it.

"One night the guy came over to our house and slit all the tires on my dad's Dodge Dart. He loved that car more than life itself."

Here we go, Sam thought.

"As soon as he replaced the tires, my dad drove over to the butcher shop and had a long talk with your grandfather. Everyone knew he worked for the Bongino family. I don't know what kind of deal they worked out, or what it cost, but the next thing I knew, our neighbor was on his knees begging my dad to forgive him. That's when I knew I wanted to work for the mob."

"You wanted to be a mobster because they threatened your neighbor?" Sam couldn't imagine how that would inspire anyone to want to join their ranks.

"You're missing the point. Unlike the cops, your grandfather got justice for my family. He didn't make excuses for the guy or tell us that we needed to learn how to get along with the man. He just handled the situation and made sure it never happened again."

"How do you justify what they do?" Sam felt bad for asking the question, but she needed to hear the answer. "I know my dad isn't a saint. He's had a lot of people killed over the years. Doesn't that bother you?"

"I've known your father since he and I were teenagers. As far as I know, he's never had an innocent person killed. I'm not saying they were guilty of the crime they were killed for, but there's no doubt in my mind, they were guilty of something."

"But you were a prosecutor. You know that sometimes innocent people get blamed for something they didn't do."

Carol chuckled. "I met a few innocent people in my life. It's not hard to tell the difference between them and a true criminal."

"Are you saying that you never sent an innocent man to jail?" Sam asked, remembering why her friend Susan had quit the district attorney's office.

"Never. A few innocent people got arrested, but none of them were ever prosecuted. You have to understand that cops almost never come into contact with an innocent person, unless they're the victim of a crime."

"I've arrested innocent people," Sam said. "Not on purpose, but it happens. I remember this one time, right after I became a cop, I was responding to a liquor store robbery when I saw someone matching the suspect's description walking down the street. Before the guy knew what was happening, I had him cuffed and in the backseat of my cruiser."

"Then what happened?"

"I took him back to the liquor store and asked the

clerk to ID him. Once we determined it wasn't him, we let him go."

"See, you're proving my point. Innocent people don't go to jail. Like I said earlier, they may not have committed the crime they were found guilty of, but they did something to end up on the cop's radar. Haven't you ever met someone that you knew was a criminal the moment you laid eyes on them?"

"Just because someone looks like a criminal doesn't make them one," Sam said, repeating the quote she had been told over and over again while she was in the academy. "Profiling isn't an accurate way to determine if someone is a criminal or not."

"Tell that lie to someone else," Carol replied with a roll of her eyes. "It may not prove right one hundred percent of the time, but it will net you far more criminals than it does innocent people."

As much as Sam hated to admit it, Carol was right. Stereotypes existed for a reason. She didn't like to use them because innocent people did get caught up in a profile, and in her opinion, no innocent person should be made to suffer.

"Let me ask you this." Carol spun around and pointed at the monitor that covered the street in front of the bar. "See the bikes. What are the odds of the owners being criminals?"

Sam studied the motorcycles for a few seconds, then shook her head. She didn't want to answer the question because it was obvious to anyone who had ever seen a member of a motorcycle gang.

"That's what I thought." The bar owner turned her attention back to Sam. "Whether or not you agree with it, profiling works. I guarantee if you walked across the street and arrested those men, you'd find out that each and every one of them were guilty of something."

"We're getting off topic," Sam said, wishing she had never brought it up. "I was asking how you felt about working for my father."

"That's easy. I couldn't imagine doing anything else."

Chapter 17

As the former assistant district attorney explained the benefits of working with the mob, Sam noted that she never mentioned money. It was as if it had played no role in her decision. That threw Sam for a loop. If anyone would have asked her what the motivation was, she would have said, "cash." In her experience, most broke the law because they thought it would benefit their bank account.

"I was thirteen when I started making deliveries for your grandfather," Carol said. The smile on her face told the rest of the story. "Back then, things were different. All of the neighborhoods were controlled by the Bongino family. You didn't have to worry about anything."

Sam did remember what that was like. When she was little, no one she knew locked their doors at night. There was no crime in her neighborhood. The street thugs knew better than to target anyone who lived under Tony Carlucci's protection.

"Right after I graduated from high school, I went to work for your father. By then, he had already put his own crew together. I could tell right away that he was going to take over the family one day. He was so smart. Within a month, we were all making more money than we had ever seen before."

"Right there," Sam said, interrupting Carol. "That's what I'm talking about. How did you sleep at night knowing that you were breaking the law?"

"We were giving the people what they wanted. If we didn't do it, someone else would have. Take drugs for example. An addict will do whatever it takes to get their next hit. All we did was save them a trip across town."

Sam could tell that she wasn't getting anywhere. Carol had been involved in the business for so long, she could no longer see the harm it caused.

"Your problem is that you see everything in black

and white. Let me tell you, there's a lot of grey in between."

"So why did you become a prosecutor?"

"It was your father's idea. Back then, women weren't allowed to be part of a crew. Sure, your grandfather and father made an exception for me, but even that took a lot of guts. Anyway, after I graduated from high school, I went to work for your father and that's when he saw a way for me to help without all the risk."

Sam realized that Carol's story mirrored her own. When her father had found out he was having a girl, he developed a plan for her to help the family without becoming a member of it. But things had changed. For the first time in her life, she was able to make the choice.

"Do you think I should give up my life and take over the business?" Sam asked, thinking the woman would state the obvious.

"You're the only one who can make that decision. I can tell you what I would do if the choice were mine." Carol leaned back and ran her fingers through her hair. "But I'm not you. I grew up in this life. It's all I know.

Without it, I'd still be in Cherry Hill, New Jersey, praying that someone would come along and change my life."

"Cherry Hill isn't that bad," Sam said, thinking back on the fond memories she had of the place.

"Tell that to my sister. You know what she's doing right now?"

Please don't say that she's waiting for someone to come along and change her life. Sam thought.

"She's working a dead-end job, and then she goes home to a man who couldn't give a crap if she lived or died. No money. No dreams. Nothing."

Although Sam didn't plan on asking the question, it slipped out of her mouth before she could stop it. She was dying to know why the bar owner hadn't done anything to help her sister get a leg up in life.

"I tried," Carol said, staring up at the ceiling. "I can't tell you how many times I asked her to leave that piece of garbage husband of hers and come live with me. It's like that old saying. You can lead a horse to water, but if it won't drink, all you can do is put two in the back of its head and call it a day."

Despite herself, Sam burst out laughing. "I don't think that's the way it goes."

Neither spoke for a few minutes. Carol was in her own world, while Sam weighed her options. There was a lot to be gained if she joined the family. Money. Security. Respect. There were also many downsides. Topping the list was the threat of spending the rest of her life behind bars.

Sam knew that if she ever came out and told the world who she was, there'd be plenty of people who made it their life's mission to put her in prison. Not because she had broken the law, but because she had managed to fool them.

"I'm not sure that I can give up being Sam Wright."

"What's so good about it?" Carol asked. "The lack of real friends? The lousy pay? If you ask me, you got the short end of the stick."

"I make a difference." Sam paused as she considered how to explain her statement. "Didn't you enjoy being a prosecutor?"

"Sure I did. But I never had the choice to do anything else and still be a part of the family. You have the opportunity to do something that's never been done before. In the history of the mafia, no woman has ever sat at the table, let alone be the boss."

"I heard there was a woman down in Florida who had her own crew once. Ran coke out of Miami for like a decade."

"That's not the same thing." Carol rolled her eyes as she shook her head. "Being a drug dealer isn't anything like being a mobster. Sure, they kill people and make a lot of money, but there's no honor. No history. Those people come and go. They're never remembered."

"That's true."

Although Sam understood what the woman was getting at, she still couldn't imagine herself as the head of the Bongino family.

"Just think about what you could do if you took over the family."

"I know the first thing I'd do," Sam said. "On day one, I'd change the name. Vittorio Bongino died in the thirties."

"Do you have any idea how proud your father would be if you changed the name?"

Sam did. She also knew that if she let Paul or Chris take over the family it would never happen. "You're not making this easy on me."

"If life were easy, we'd all be sitting poolside with a glass of Campari in our hand."

"Ain't that the truth," Sam said, getting out of her chair. "I better get going. I still have to swap cars before I head to the city."

Chapter 18

The sun was sitting just above the Pacific Ocean when Sam turned into her father's neighborhood. She had always loved that time of day. When the hustle and bustle of the city had quieted, and the sounds of nature took over. Unlike other major cities around the country, San Francisco didn't operate twenty-four hours per day, seven days per week. If you knew where to look, you could find peace and quiet after the sun had finished its trek across the sky.

Off in the distance, Sam spotted a cruise ship bound for parts unknown. Alaska perhaps, or maybe Hawaii. She envied the people on board. They weren't forced to contemplate their lives the way she was. None of them had spent their lives living as someone else or were forced to choose between the two existences.

The thought ended when she pulled up to the gate separating her father's home from his neighbors. Sam knew that most of the people living in the neighborhood had no clue they were living within a stone's throw of the most powerful mobster the country had ever known. She was sure they would have moved if they had.

For all the good that Tony Carlucci did, there was a side of him that put the fear of God into normal people. Since becoming a made man, Tony had killed or ordered the deaths of more than a thousand souls. His utter disregard for life was well known worldwide. That was what had propelled him to the head of the Bongino family.

Keeping her hands in plain view, Sam watched as the guard approached her vehicle. Although she couldn't see the gun underneath his suit jacket, she was sure it was there. More guards would be watching her from the deepening shadows. If she did anything stupid at that point, she'd die in a hail of gunfire.

"Good evening," the guard said to her. His eyes

shifted from her to the backseat, then the storage area at the rear of her Subaru. When he was satisfied that she was alone, he tilted his head toward the wrought iron gate. As if by magic, the sound of an electric motor sprang to life and opened the gate. "Please park next to the garage," he said, as she put the car into gear. The routine was always the same.

The second that Sam stepped out of her car; she saw the front doors of the mansion swing open. Although she was backlit, Sam could tell it was her mother. The woman could hear like a bat.

Just get it over with, Sam told herself, as she got out of her car.

Anastasia didn't move until Sam climbed the steps. Then, like a jungle cat, she pounced, wrapping her arms around her daughter as if they hadn't seen each other in years.

"Benvenuti a casa," she said, pulling Sam into the house. "Dinner will be ready in one hour."

Sam didn't have it in her to tell her mother that she wasn't hungry. Not that it would have made a difference.

Anastasia would make her eat anyway. The woman believed that all of the world's problems could be solved if more people just sat down to a decent meal on a regular basis.

"Is dad here?" Sam asked.

"Dove altro sarebbe?" Anastasia held Sam out at arm's length and looked her up and down as if trying to decide whether or not she was worthy to have an audience with her father. "He's in his office."

Leaning forward, Sam gave her mother a kiss, then headed down the long hallway that led to the back of the home. She didn't bother looking at the new paintings or tapestries that adorned the walls. As pretty as they were, she needed to speak with her father before she lost her nerve.

Tony looked up as she tapped on the doorframe. As usual, the mob boss sat at his desk, sipping scotch from a glass made out of crystal. Standing up, he embraced his daughter, then motioned for her to sit.

"How are things in Camden?" he asked.

Sam hated it when her father tried to make small talk. For all his strengths, that was one area in which he knew nothing about. Every time he tried; all it did was make her uncomfortable. She knew that he didn't do it with other people.

"I was wondering if you could help me with the case that I'm working on? I've got nothing, and if I don't solve this case, everyone's going to know that I'm a fraud."

"You worry too much, Samorn. You're the best detective in the bay area and everyone knows it. You should hear the way the cops around here talk about you."

For a second, Sam didn't know what to say. While she was well aware that some of the cops in the north bay talked about her success rate, she had no idea that word of her abilities had stretched all the way down into the city. The idea both thrilled and scared her.

Taking his seat, Tony asked her what kind of help she needed. They both knew that he would do whatever it took to make sure she succeeded, even if that meant forcing someone to confess to the crime.

Knowing that her father would have heard about the case, Sam didn't bother with the details. What she needed was to speak with someone who might have an idea as to why Aaron Burwell had been killed, or who did it.

"When did he get whacked?"

"On or about July fourth, nineteen ninety-nine. The cops assumed he had left town on his own, so they didn't bother investigating his disappearance."

"I heard he was found underneath some cops' house. Could he have done it?"

As much as Sam would have loved to pin the murder on Sgt. Edwards, she knew he hadn't done it. At best, he helped cover up the crime. At worst, he was just an incompetent fool who should have never been permitted to carry a gun and a badge.

"No one was living in the house when the body was placed in the crawlspace. It had been sitting empty for a while."

"What's that got to do with anything?" Tony asked. "The cop knew the place was empty, right? What better place to dispose of a body than a house you know no one is going to break into? If you ask me, it's the perfect hiding place."

"My gut tells me he's not involved."

"Who else wanted this guy killed?"

"That's the million-dollar question." Sam got up and poured herself a glass of scotch. "Do you know who was in charge of that area twenty-five years ago?"

Chapter 19

"To the best of my knowledge, none of the families were working in the north bay back then. Old man Bongino ran the lumber mills back in the day, but I think that was further north."

Sam had been expecting that answer. Even today, Camden was too small to attract the attention of any of the mafia families. If she hadn't moved there to become a cop, her father would have never wasted the time to pick the city out on a map.

"If you want, I can ask around," Tony said. "But I'd be surprised if anyone knows anything about this kid getting killed. Did he owe money to anyone?"

"Not that I know of." Sam drank the rest of her

scotch, then stared up at the ceiling hoping that the answer would present itself to her. "I just don't know where to begin."

Tony leaned forward and placed his elbows on the desk. "Start with why the kid was killed."

Thanks, Captain Obvious, she thought.

"This kid was some kind of star athlete, right? Maybe someone on his team thought he was getting too much attention, or it could have been someone on an opposing team who didn't like that he was beating them all the time."

"Maybe," Sam said, still thinking that someone had murdered him because the games were rigged. "There are just too many suspects." She picked up her glass, then sat it back down when she realized it was empty. "According to my neighbor, half the town was betting on his games."

"So you're thinking someone whacked this kid over money?" Tony rubbed his chin for a few seconds as he considered it. "People have been known to kill over money."

"I know." Sam wondered how many people her father had sent to the grave because of some debt they owed the family. "They were rigging the games."

"That means someone was making a lot of money. Do you know who was doing it?"

"Not a clue," she said, as she got up and walked to the bar. "I just know it happened. The kid only lost one game."

As Sam poured herself another drink, she remembered what the lieutenant had said about the gambling angle. While it may have been easy to determine the outcome of a high school football game, it would have been impossible to do that once the kid went to college.

Or is it? She asked herself.

Turning around, Sam asked her father how hard it was to rig college football. The moment he smiled; she had her answer. Then it dawned on her that it might be easy for someone like her father to do it, but no one in Camden possessed his power.

As if he could read her mind, Tony explained that there were multiple ways to get the outcome you wanted when it came to sports.

"Maybe he gets hurt before a big game. Maybe the quarterback on the other team finds out his parents are going to lose their house if he has a good game. Trust me, it's not that hard to influence who wins and loses."

"No one in Camden has that kind of power," Sam said, feeling like she had just lost her best chance of solving the case.

"Okay. Then maybe they only bet on the games they know he's going to lose."

"That's possible." As the idea made laps inside her head, Sam realized that it wouldn't work. If Aaron threw too many games, he'd either be benched or cut from the team. "What else could he do to make sure they lost?"

"There are hundreds of ways to lose. If he didn't want to pay someone to have a bad game, he could spike their drink or something the night before."

While it made sense, Sam still couldn't make the math add up in her head. There were too many variables to consider. Plus, the whole thing relied on Aaron going along with the plan. She made a mental note to check out the college Aaron had planned on attending. If it were a small school with no hopes of getting national coverage, she'd have to shelve her idea and look into another reason why he might have been killed.

Sam was about to ask another question, when she remembered the way that the mayor had been acting while she was in his office. Changing the subject, she asked her father if he'd consider giving her the information the family had gathered on the mayor.

"That's not a good idea," Tony said. "If you got caught with it, there'd be no way to explain why you had it or where you had gotten the information."

"Can you at least tell me what kind of guy he was when he was young?"

Tony's eyes narrowed as he considered her request. "You think he might have had something to do with this murder case you're working on?"

Although Sam wanted to say no, she knew it was never wise to lie to her father. "He was acting kind of shifty when I went to see him about the card game."

"Interesting." The mob boss leaned back in his chair and started rubbing his chin again. "From what we could gather, the mayor was a bit of a wild child, if you know what I mean. He like to get drunk on the weekends, then go street racing."

Sam couldn't picture the mayor being a rowdy teenager. "Did he ever get busted?"

"Several times. The only thing that kept him out of jail was his family's money. He's related to the people who founded Camden. They still own a bunch of land over in Napa."

I wonder if Aaron was into the street racing scene, Sam thought. While it was a long shot, she could imagine a race leading to a fight, then an accidental murder. It wasn't out of the realm of possibilities. Glancing at the clock on the wall, Sam realized they were late for dinner.

"We better stop before mom sends one of the guards to get us."

Chapter 20

As the family ate, Sam allowed herself to consider the possibility that Aaron had been murdered for some reason other than money. Everyone else in her department thought it boiled down to jealousy or revenge. Although both were viable options, she couldn't see it. In her experience, it always came back to money.

"Dad, have you ever…" Sam stopped herself before the words could come out of her mouth. Not only was it inappropriate to ask why he had murdered people, business was never discussed at the dinner table.

Anastasia shot her a dirty look, then mumbled something about ungrateful children under her breath.

"Never mind," Sam said, thinking she could find out

the answer by asking one of her cousins. Both of them were as cold blooded as her father, but at the same time, were more open to discuss business now that they knew she was considering taking over the family one day.

Feeling like she had crossed the line, Sam ate in silence until her father brought up his brother's upcoming wedding.

"He's planning on getting married the week before Christmas," Tony said.

"Christmas?" Anastasia asked. "Per amore di tutte le cose sante. What kind of man would get married on the day our Lord was born?"

Sam thought about pointing out that Jesus had been born in the summer but knew it would only cause her mother to turn her anger on her.

"He's getting married the week before," Tony said, like it made any difference. "He wants to wait until after the merger."

There was no reason to ask what merger. Her uncle was marrying Liliana Gigliotti. She was the daughter of Gino Gigliotti, the man who ran the Marchetti family. A small outfit out of northern New Jersey. Once the pair were married, the Marchetti's would fall under her father's protection and would no longer have to report to the families in New York.

"I thought you were going to wait until after they were married," Sam asked, wondering why the merger was happening first.

"Samorn!" Anastasia slammed her hand on the table, rattling the silverware on their plates. "We do not discuss business at the dinner table."

"I was…" Sam nodded, then apologized. "You're right, mother." She turned to her father and asked where the wedding was to be held.

"Sicily," Tony replied, with more than a little pride in his voice. "They're getting married in the same church where all Carlucci men have taken their vows."

That's not what I was told, Sam said to herself. Last she had heard; the pair were planning on getting married in Vegas at one of the casino's run by the family. Assuming that her father had played some role in the decision to change venues, she kept her mouth shut.

"Ricardo is taking a year off to spend with his new bride," Tony stated, before turning to Sam. "This means that I have to select someone to take his place while he is gone."

"Anthony. What did I just say?" Anastasia asked, in a rare moment of defiance. "There is to be no talk of business at my table."

"Forgive me, il mio amore." Tony reached over and took her hand. "I'm just excited about the prospect of my daughter taking her rightful place at my side."

"I don't care. I don't want any more talk of this at my table."

Sam was stunned into silence. While it wasn't unusual for her mother to tell other people not to discuss business outside of her father's office, she had never seen the woman tell her father to stop. The move disturbed her. From the day she was born, her mother had been submissive to the point of revulsion. Sam had always told herself it was because Anastasia believed in the old ways. Now, Sam didn't know what to think. When her mother left the room, Sam saw her chance.

"What was that about?"

"Your mother thinks that I've made a terrible decision by allowing you to decide what you want to do with the rest of your life."

"Of course she does," Sam whispered. "She's been wanting me to get married and pump out a bunch of kids since the day I learned how to walk."

The mobster leaned forward and warned Sam not to disrespect her mother. The implication was clear. Sam was his only child, but he had sworn before God to love and honor his wife until the day he died.

"I didn't mean any disrespect." Sam bowed her head. She was well aware that she had crossed the line. "What's she going to say if I decide to join the family?"

"Let me worry about that," he said, keeping one eye on the door that separated the dining room from the kitchen. "Have you decided what you want to do?"

If he had asked her the day before, Sam would have said that she wanted to remain a cop. Sitting there with him seated at the head of the table, she wasn't so sure. "I don't know what I want."

"I understand." Tony wiped his mouth with the napkin, then excused himself to go check on his wife.

Sam cursed herself for being a coward. *I should have just told him no.*

As the thought settled in her mind, she realized why the words had not come out of her mouth. Part of her wanted to take the reins. To be the first woman to lead an Italian mafia family was something anyone in their right mind would jump at the chance to do.

What are you thinking?

The days of the mafia were drawing to an end, and no one knew that better than Sam. As a cop, she had seen how the government had shifted their focus from the mob families to terrorists. Despite what her father believed; the good old days were never coming back. In another few years, there would be no such thing as the mafia.

Chapter 21

As soon as dinner was over, Sam made the excuse that she was tired and wanted to go home. While she wasn't sure if her parents believed her or not, it got her out of the house. She suspected they weren't too disappointed by her departure. Their dinner conversation had spoiled the mood long before she decided to leave.

On the drive back to the north bay, Sam considered the other options for Aaron's death. Instead of taking the exit which led to her house, she followed the freeway until she reached Rohnert Park. Following Golf Course Drive, Sam reached her destination.

Fifteen minutes to spare, Sam thought, as she headed into the frozen yogurt shop.

Over the years, she had found their Very Berry smoothie relaxing. Somehow, the concoction helped her think. Not wanting to delay their closing, she took the sweet drink outside and sat down at one of the small tables which provided her a view of the golf course across the street.

Off in the distance, she heard an engine racing. The sound had become very common over the last few years as police budgets were slashed. Less money meant fewer cops on the street. And while she agreed that some aspects of policing needed to change, the activists who were bent on defunding the agencies refused to see the effect they were having on the communities they were trying to help.

A moment later, a modern muscle car came into view. In her estimation, it was traveling at twice the posted speed limit. Part of her wondered how long it would be before the driver either killed himself or someone else.

Returning to her drink, Sam thought about what her father had said about the mayor having been involved in street racing when he was younger. Coupled with his love for drinking, she could see how the two could have gotten the man into trouble.

Is it possible that he was the one who had struck Aaron? Sam asked herself.

Although she had thought the accident had been a result of him losing an important football game, she had to admit there were some other angles to consider.

"Are you going to be much longer?"

Sam spun around and stared at the frozen yogurt shop employee. "No," she said, hopping up off the bench.

Walking over to the nearest trash can, Sam tossed what was left of her drink into the receptacle, then made her way over to the Subaru. No matter how hard she tried, Sam couldn't get the image of the mayor's reaction to the news that they had found Aaron out of her mind.

What she had told her father was true. She didn't think the guy had killed the teenager, but she was sure he knew something about it.

The list of possible reasons was long. The mayor could have witnessed the murder. He could have heard it was being planned. Maybe a friend had confessed to killing the kid.

Or maybe he found the body. Sam thought. *Someone took the watch.*

Twisting the key, Sam waited a few seconds for the engine to settle down before she put the car in drive and turned toward the exit. Like it or not, she was going to have to speak to the mayor again.

But how?

Sam knew that she couldn't just come out and accuse the man of being involved. While she wasn't worried about him retaliating against her, the thought of him acting out did give her pause. Desperate people would often do stupid things without considering the consequence of their actions.

Not only could he lead a revolt against her, but he could also use his authority to hurt the department. As mayor, he had a great deal of influence over their budget. With a stroke of his pen, he could ensure they had what they needed or take it away.

Her first thought was to use the gambling ring against him. Although he hadn't revitalized it yet, he had been putting the pieces together.

"Don't go there," Sam told herself.

As effective as blackmail was, she didn't want to use it against anyone unless there was no other choice. Taking away someone's ability to decide things for themselves seemed more than wrong to her. Sam knew that if somebody tried that with her, she'd kill them without giving it a second thought.

Sam was still considering her options when she spotted red and blue lights flashing in the distance. Slowing down, she changed lanes, hoping the local cops had found the speeder and was now in the process of taking him to jail. As she passed by the scene, her heart sank.

Although the officers had done their best to block the view of passing motorists, Sam could see the corner of the sheet being used to cover the body. Not seeing any other cars around, she assumed that whoever had hit the pedestrian had driven off instead of hanging around to help the victim.

The voice in the back of her head told her to keep driving. She was still four miles from her jurisdiction.

Besides, it wasn't like she had the ability to raise the person from the dead. Plus, she could always call the Rohnert Park Police in the morning to see if they had any idea who may have run the person over.

Sam pulled to the side of the road as soon as she saw the ambulance approaching. While she waited for it to pass, she reconsidered her decision to go home. Having worked hit and runs before, she knew the effect it was having on the officers and if nothing else, she thought she might offer to go grab them some coffee while they conducted their investigation.

"Stop being stupid," Sam told herself. "They don't need your help."

Easing her foot off the brake pedal, Sam took one last look at the accident scene, then focused on what lay ahead of her.

Chapter 22

Bright and early the next morning, Sam walked across the street and rang Christine's doorbell. As much as she hated to wake the woman up, she needed her help if she was going to get Megan talking.

A full minute passed before the retired nurse opened the door. She looked as if she had been dragged down two miles of bad road. The dark circles beneath her eyes relayed the message that she had gone without sleep the night before.

"I knew you were coming," Christine said, giving Sam room to enter the house. "Megan's lawyer doesn't want me talking to you."

For a second, Sam didn't know what to say. If she

were in the lawyer's shoes, she'd have done the same thing. In spite of their rocky relationship, Christine's opinion still mattered to Megan.

When they reached the kitchen, Sam spotted a notepad lying on the counter next to the phone. A line had been drawn down the center of the page. On one side, it listed the pros of helping, and on the other, the cons. It wasn't hard to tell which way Christine was leaning.

"If you'd rather not talk about it, I'll understand," Sam said, taking a seat at the small table.

"It's not your fault." Christine lumbered over to the coffee maker and pressed the brew button, bringing the machine to life. "I always knew that sooner or later Megan would find herself sitting in a jail cell. She's not like my other girls."

Sam knew that was true. The other two children were successful and leading productive lives. One had followed her mother's footsteps and was working as a nurse at the children's hospital in San Francisco. The youngest had gotten into computers and was now creating apps to help people better manage their time.

Handing the first cup to Sam, Christine explained

that she had done her best to raise each of the girls the same way, yet despite her best efforts, the middle child had chosen to blaze a trail of her own.

"It happens," Sam said. "I see it all the time."

In an instant, Sam could tell that just because it happened to other people, it didn't make Christine feel any better. The woman needed something more than platitudes. She needed answers to explain how one of her children turned out to be a rotten apple.

The truth of the situation was that no one knew why it happened. How could kids raised in the same home by the same parents turn out so different?

Feeling like it would be better to change the subject, Sam asked Christine if she remembered what the mayor was like as a young man.

"That boy was always in trouble," she replied. "When he was fourteen, he stole his daddy's car and drove to San Francisco. He might have gotten away with it if he had known how to read a gas gauge. The boy ran out of gas, right in the middle of the Golden Gate Bridge."

While it was idiotic, Sam had been hoping for

worse. Something that would be an indicator of future violence perhaps.

Christine pressed her lips together for a few seconds while she searched her memory. "A year or so later, he got it in his head to drive onto the football field and do donuts on the fifty-yard line."

"How'd he get caught?"

"His car got stuck in the grass. He showed up around an hour after the groundskeepers had left. They had just finished spraying the field for that weekend's game."

Now we're getting somewhere, Sam thought. She had already known about his fascination with cars. Getting in trouble for tearing up the football field may have made him want to get back at the school.

"What else?" Christine asked herself, as she tapped her coffee cup. "Oh yeah. The street racing. Back in the day, all the kids would go out to Berry Road and see how fast their cars would go. A half dozen kids or more lost their lives on that road before they started shutting it down."

Sam tried to picture the scene in her mind. "Do you remember what section of the road they raced on?"

"The whole thing. Back then, there were only a few houses on that road. It wasn't until two thousand six that they started building anything out there. I remember when the city first proposed the idea."

The retired nurse went on with her story, but Sam wasn't listening. If Berry Road was where all the local kids went to drag race, that meant the mayor had been near the house on more than one occasion. Anyone with half a brain would have known it was empty.

Crimes required two elements. Motive and opportunity. Sam could prove the mayor had the opportunity. He knew the location well. All she had to do was prove he was somewhere near Berry Road the night that Aaron went missing.

What about motive? Sam asked herself. The two were more than a few years apart in age. *Why would someone in their mid-twenties want to kill someone fresh out of high school?*

There was no answer. Unless she could prove that Aaron liked to street race or at least go out and watch them, she was short on motive. The idea was still bouncing around inside her head when she realized that Christine was still talking.

Catching the end of the sentence, Sam assumed the retired nurse was referring to the mayor's drinking habit. Not wanting to give away that she hadn't been listening, Sam turned around and looked at the clock on the wall.

"I better get to work," she said, getting to her feet. "Thanks for the coffee."

"Any time," Christine replied. "Before you go." The woman slid out of the chair, then motioned for Sam to follow her. When they reached the end of the hallway, she asked Sam to go inside. "Megan's diary is in the top drawer."

"I can't take that." Sam started to back out of the room.

"Yes you can. This is my house and I give you permission to take anything you want." Christine blocked the exit. "She kept diaries all the way up through high school. The one in the top drawer is from her senior year. I know that, because on the first page, she talks about a date she went on with Aaron."

Sam turned and looked at the dresser. Although

every fiber of her being told her that it should be okay to take the twenty-five-year-old diary, she couldn't bring herself to do it. If it linked Megan to the crime, they'd have a problem. That's when she explained that she'd have to check with the D.A. before touching it.

Pushing past her, Christine retrieved the diary, then handed it to Sam. "Get it out of my house before I read it. I know that she was never an angel, but I don't want to know…"

"I'll take it," Sam said, to keep the woman from having to finish the sentence.

Chapter 23

At every stop light, Sam glanced over at the diary wondering if she should have agreed to take it with her. It was like having Pandora's box lying in the seat next to her. Despite her feeling that it was okay to possess the book, she couldn't bring herself to open it.

How do you manage to always get yourself into this position? Sam asked herself.

A horn blaring from somewhere behind her pulled her attention back to the present. Letting her foot off the brake, Sam looked both ways before driving through the intersection.

By the time she reached the station, Sam was ready to explode. Grabbing the diary, she made her way into the building, passed the men and women who were gathered in the bull pen waiting to begin their shift. Although she knew it wasn't possible, she felt like they knew she was walking a legal tightrope.

Spotting Jenna near the break room, Sam changed direction and started toward her supervisor waiving the diary around as if it held the secrets of the universe.

"What's that?" Jenna asked, keeping her eyes on her coffee as she stirred the cream into it.

"Megan Johnson's diary. Her mom gave it to me." Sam wasn't surprised when the sergeant took a step backward. "It's from her senior year in high school."

"Have you looked at it yet?" Jenna looked at the diary like it was a venomous snake ready to strike.

"I'm waiting for Marsha to send over the search warrant. She says we're good, but I thought it would be better to wait. Even though it was in Christine's house, it still belongs to Megan."

"I'm not sure how that works. If you want to get technical about it, we could argue that Megan abandoned it when she moved out." The sergeant paused to take a sip of her coffee. "There's something else we need to consider. What if something in there implicates her in the murder?"

Sam had been thinking the same thing. While remote, it was still something they had to consider. The last thing the district attorney needed was to have the evidence tossed out, all because she had failed to get a warrant for the diary.

"My gut tells me that she wasn't involved."

"Are you willing to let her walk if you're wrong?" Jenna asked. "For now, I say we put it away until Marsha sends the warrant over."

"Fair enough," Sam replied. Tucking the diary under her arm, she fed four quarters into the soda machine and punched the button to release a Pepsi. "There's something else I want to talk to you about." She looked to make sure they were alone, then mentioned the mayor might be involved.

The sergeant looked at her as if she had lost her mind. "We'll talk about this in my office."

As they walked toward the detective's wing of the building, Sam thought about all the ways her suspicion could come back and blow up in their faces. She had gotten lucky when she had brought down the city councilmen and county supervisors. Unlike then, she had nothing but an opinion linking the mayor to the Burwell case.

Once they were inside the office, Jenna shut the door and asked Sam to take a seat. Neither one of them could afford to have someone overhear their conversation.

"Lay it out for me," the sergeant said, taking a seat behind her desk.

Sam wasn't sure where to start. The lines connecting the mayor to the case were tenuous at best. He was far from the only person in town who had loved to drag race back in the day. Then there was the football angle. While he may have been upset with the school staff, there was no reason for him to go after the star quarterback years after he had gotten caught tearing up the field.

When Sam started to open her mouth to explain her theory, she realized that she had no reason to explain why she had gone to see the mayor in the first place. He wasn't part of any investigation they were working on.

"Spit it out already," Jenna said.

"I ran into the mayor yesterday. I needed to talk to him about the new dog park in my neighborhood." Sam paused to replay that sentence in her mind. Deciding it was good enough, she continued. "While I was there, he asked how the Burwell case was going."

"That doesn't surprise me. He's always asking about the cases we're working on. I think it's his way of justifying how much money the city gives us each year."

"I get that he's nosey, but…" Sam wasn't sure how to explain it. "You know the mayor, right?" She gave Jenna a chance to nod. "He's one of the worst liars I've ever met."

"Go on."

"When I told him that Aaron had never left town, he wasn't surprised. Not even a little." Sam was all in now. "Then I found out that he used to street race on Berry Road back in the day."

"Everyone in town knows that. We all drag raced on Berry Road until they built the new shopping center and put up that stupid red light."

Sam started to back pedal. "I'm not saying he killed Aaron, but I think he knows who did. Like I said, he's a terrible liar."

"Do you know where he was that night?"

"He was never interviewed," Sam replied. "I just wanted to give you a heads up before I started looking into his past."

"I'm fine with you asking him about it, but make sure his name isn't brought up to anyone else unless you have proof he was involved. We don't need him as an enemy. I don't know if you're aware of this or not, but his family has more money than God."

"I understand."

Chapter 24

When Sam came out of the office, she saw Amy sitting at her desk, talking on the phone. The detective had a huge smile on her face. Placing one hand over the receiver, she waved Sam over.

"I may have found something," she said. "Tim Creighton has an assault conviction in San Benito County. Guess who was with him at the time?"

Sam didn't need to guess. She was more interested as to why Sgt. Edwards hadn't been charged at the time. Her gut told her it was because he was on the job, but she hoped that she was wrong. While it wasn't unusual for one cop to look the other way for a fellow law enforcement officer, she liked to believe that an assault would trump any sense of loyalty one might feel for another.

Sensing the question, Amy explained that no one could place the former cop at the scene when the fight broke out. While the deputy who had responded to the call suspected the sergeant was involved, he had nothing to confirm his suspicion, so he was forced to drop the matter.

"Did Creighton do any time?" Sam asked, hoping he had. If so, she planned on using it against the man when it came time to question him about Aaron's death.

"Just probation." Amy held up a finger to cut Sam off. Turning back to the call, she mumbled something, then thanked the person before hanging up. "Okay. Here's what I found out."

The detective repeated everything she had learned from the D.A. down in Hollister. The pair had gone down to the once active farming town in order to watch the local football team take on the state champs. While the excuse sounded odd, even then, no one could prove otherwise.

After the game, Tim Creighton had chosen to ex-press his opinion of the game with the coach of the opposing team. When the coach tried to walk away, Tim took a swing. By the time the deputies arrived to break it up, more than thirty people were fighting.

"Who in their right mind drives three hours to watch a high school football game?" Sam asked, trying to figure out what had inspired the men to go to Hollister in the first place. "Any family down there?"

"Not that I can find," Amy replied. "At the time, they claimed they were coming back from a fishing trip and decided to stop off and see the game."

"When did this happen?"

"A couple of weeks before Aaron got run over."

Sam dropped into the chair next to Amy's desk as she considered the possibilities as to why the men had gone to the game. There was only one explanation she could come up with.

"We need to find out if there were any scouts at the game. You said the state champs were playing, right?"

"Yeah, but that still doesn't explain why Edwards and Creighton would drive all the way down there. As far as I know, Aaron wasn't with them."

"Maybe they took a tape with them. Or maybe they were trying to convince the scout to come up to Camden to watch him play."

Amy nodded, then jotted something down in her notebook. "I'll see what I can come up with." Her eyes shifted over to the sergeant's door. "What were you talking to Jenna about?"

Looking over her shoulder to make sure the door was still closed; Sam explained her hypothesis about the mayor being involved in the case. As she spoke, she could tell the detective wasn't buying it. Not that she blamed her. As far as ideas went, it was pretty bad.

"From what I've heard, he was just a kid who liked to party and have a good time," Amy said. "I can't see him killing someone."

"What if it was an accident?" Sam asked. "What if he and his friends were out drinking and driving and somehow they ran across Aaron walking down the side of the road and hit him with their car?"

"Anything's possible, but someone would have heard about it. If you run somebody over, there's evidence of it. Skid marks. A broken headlight. Besides,

Aaron was beaten to death, not run over."

Sam leaned back and ran her fingers through her hair. Amy had a point. Whoever had killed Aaron had used a baseball bat or something similar. "What if he was killed because he remembered who ran him over?"

"If he figured out who had run him over, why not go to the cops?"

"Maybe he thought blackmailing the person was a better option. Think about it. Aaron gets run over right after he loses the biggest game of his life. What if like everyone else, he thought it was someone who was upset about the game? Then a couple of months later, he finds out that it was just some idiot out with his friends drinking and driving."

"Let's say you're right and the mayor ran him over and broke his leg. Why kill him? Why not go to daddy and have him pay the kid off?"

"Maybe he did, but Aaron wanted more money? Christine told me that Aaron had decided to stop playing football. It's possible he made that decision because he knew he'd never have to worry about money again."

"It should be easy enough to find out if the mayor

was involved. All we need to do is find out what he was driving when Aaron got run over. Then see if anyone in town remembers seeing any damage on the car."

Feeling pretty confident that she was on the right path, Sam suggested that Amy talk to the people who worked at the local garages while she talked to the mayor's friends. If all went well, one of them would admit to the crime and they could put the case to bed before it got any colder.

"Hold up," Amy said, as Sam started to leave. "What about the watch? Why would the mayor and his friends go back for it?"

Sam wished the detective wouldn't have reminded her about it. That was the one piece of the puzzle which didn't make any sense at all. Going back and robbing a corpse of a watch spoke of someone who either valued the piece or knew it could link them to the murder. And the mayor didn't fit either of those descriptions.

"We'll worry about that later," Sam said, as she walked out of the room.

Chapter 25

Tracking down who knew the mayor twenty-five years ago proved harder than Sam had realized. After obtaining a yearbook from the high school alumni committee, Sam spent hours poring over every image which contained the mayor. From what she could tell, he was one of the most popular students in the school at the time. It wasn't much of a surprise considering he had come from a wealthy family.

"Why are you still here?" Jenna asked, as she exited her office. Before Sam could reply, she told the detective to call it a day and go home. "The case will still be here tomorrow."

"Let me run an idea by you," Sam said.

After she was done explaining her latest theory of the crime, she asked Jenna if she thought it was possible.

"It's better than someone killing him because he didn't want to play football anymore, but it still doesn't answer all of the questions."

Like Amy, the sergeant questioned why the mayor or anyone else would go back for the watch. In her opinion, the only person who would do that was someone who had ties to the it. That meant it had to be somebody related to the victim.

"I'm not giving up on Creighton yet," Sam said, knowing that it would be almost impossible to tie him to the crime. "And before you ask about the diary, Marsha still hasn't sent the warrant over yet, but she says that she got it signed."

"That's not a surprise."

They both knew how busy the acting district attorney was. Not only were they down a prosecutor, the number of cases they were working on had increased since Justin Macat had been killed. Sam felt sorry for them. It was hard enough dealing with the death of a friend, let alone the boss.

Reaching for her purse, Sam asked Jenna if she wanted to join her for a drink. Tossing back a few at their favorite watering hole had always cheered the woman up.

"I better not. The lieutenant has already warned me many times about hanging out with you guys when we're off the clock. He says that it sets a bad example."

While Sam didn't agree, she figured it wasn't worth arguing about. Not hanging out wasn't going to change their relationship. She and Jenna had been friends for more than a year before being promoted to sergeant. And while she was exceptional at her job, she was incapable of forgetting where she had come from.

"If you change your mind, feel free to stop by. I'll buy the first round."

"Speaking of which," Jenna said. "Do me a favor and park in the public lot down the street. Someone saw you there the other day and complained about it."

"No problem."

Sam gave her boss a fifteen-minute head start before she followed her out of the building. As she made her way to the Explorer, she saw Sgt. McMasters and Sienna having a conversation in the smoking area. It seemed odd considering that neither of them smoked.

Taking the chance that they weren't talking about anything important, she walked over and asked how they were doing. The two shared a look before the sergeant answered.

"Rumor has it that you went to see the mayor yesterday."

The statement didn't surprise Sam. The sergeant had called Camden home his entire life and knew everyone. What did shock her was the fact that he would bring it up.

"I went to talk to him about a personal matter," she replied, hoping he would drop the subject.

"It must have been something important. Because right after you left, he told his secretary that he was leaving for the day and wouldn't be back until Monday."

"Did you consider the possibility that my visit may not have had anything to do with why the mayor needed some time off? Maybe one of his kids got sick or something."

"I've never been a big fan of coincidences. I don't know what you said to him, but something spooked that man. I drove by his place last night before coming to work and he wouldn't answer the door. Kept telling me to mind my own business."

"He told me the same thing when I stopped by his house this morning," Sienna said. "Maybe one thing has nothing to do with the other, but you have to admit it seems a little funky that he'd go into hiding right after he talked with you."

"Fine," Sam said, knowing they wouldn't drop it until she told them the truth. "I heard that the mayor was thinking about picking up where Justin left off, so I went by to let him know that the cat was out of the bag. I didn't want him to get in over his head."

"Where did you hear that?" McMasters asked. The look on his face told Sam that he didn't believe a word of it.

"Your boyfriend told you, didn't he?" Sienna asked.

"To start with, Gary isn't my boyfriend. We're just two law enforcement officers, who on occasion, grab a drink together. Nothing more."

"And he didn't have a problem with you telling the mayor that his name came up in the course of his investigation."

"You're assuming that Gary was the one who told me," Sam replied, wishing she had just gotten into her SUV and left without talking to the pair. "As far as I know, no one is investigating the mayor for anything. All I did was tell a friend to be careful."

McMasters turned his head toward the sky and cursed the mayor for being an idiot. "I knew he was up to something." He then looked at Sam. "How bad is it?"

"I don't know. From what I heard, nothing's happened yet. I guess it was still in the planning stages." Then Sam remembered her own investigation. "He might have another problem though. His name has come up in connection with our case."

"The Burwell thing?" McMasters asked.

"Do you happen to remember what kind of car he was driving at the time of Aaron's accident?"

The sergeant shook his head as he started to walk away. "You're barking up the wrong tree, Wright. Pete Davidson isn't a murderer."

"Maybe not, but I'd bet my life that he knows what happened to Aaron on the night he disappeared."

Chapter 26

Sam took a step back as the sergeant advanced on her. Although she knew he would never strike a woman, his anger came as a surprise. In the five years she had known him, she'd never seen him lose his cool, yet there he was, ready to pick a fight.

"I've known Pete his entire life. There's no way he killed that kid."

"He knew Aaron never left town. If he didn't have anything to do with his disappearance, how'd he know that?"

The sergeant's eyes shifted from her to the parking lot, then back again. "What makes you think he knows anything about it?"

"Come on, Sarge. The mayor is the worst liar I've ever met. The second I brought up that Aaron had never left town, he freaked out. It was written all over his face."

Sam watched as the sergeant and Sienna shared a look of acknowledgement. They both knew she was telling the truth. Anyone who had ever met the mayor knew he was a terrible liar.

"I still can't believe he had anything to do with it," McMasters said. Although he was still angry, the fire inside of him was burning itself out. "Have you told Jenna about it yet?"

"I did," Sam admitted. "Look, I don't want to believe it either, but there's no doubt in my mind that he knows something. Maybe that's all it is."

"Let me talk to him."

It was all that Sam could do to keep her mouth from falling open. What the sergeant was suggesting went against every policy the department had. While officers often came into contact with people they knew, they were never allowed to talk to them about an active case. Especially when they might be a suspect.

"I can't let you do that, Sarge. The chief will fire

you in a heartbeat if he finds out that you talked to a suspect off the record."

"Isn't that what you did yesterday?"

While Sam considered the two events at opposite ends of the spectrum, she couldn't deny the charge. She had given the mayor a heads up about an investigation. Even if it wasn't the truth.

"We go way back," McMasters said. "If he had anything to do with it, he'll tell me. Then I'll convince him to turn himself in." He shook his head as Sam started to object. "I'm on my way out anyways. What can they do to me?"

"Besides take away your pension?"

"She's right," Sienna said. "If you interfere in the investigation, you could lose everything."

"It doesn't matter. If, and that's a big if, Peter was involved, he's going to need a friend in his corner. He's always been there when I needed him and now it's my turn to repay the favor."

Sam could tell that she wasn't going to talk the sergeant out of it. Like any good friend, the man was determined to do what was necessary to protect the person he cared about.

"How about this? Call and get him to meet you somewhere outside of the city limits. Go fishing or hiking or whatever. That way, if he confesses, you can say it was a spontaneous event that you had no control over."

The sergeant nodded, then reached for his phone. As the man walked away, Sam wondered how her relationship with him would end up. For all intents and purposes, she had crushed the man's spirit by telling him that one of his oldest friends might be a murderer.

"How sure are you about this?" Sienna asked.

"That he did it or that he knows who did?" Sam waited to make sure the sergeant was out of earshot. "I'm one hundred percent sure he knows what happened the night Aaron disappeared. As to whether or not he was involved, I don't know."

"Walk me through it."

Sam laid out her theory, starting with the idea that it had been an accident brought on by drinking or driving too fast. By the time she was finished, she could tell that Sienna was convinced. At least enough to say it warranted further investigation.

The cop ran a hand over her face before she pulled her phone out of her pocket. Swiping her thumb across the screen, she showed Sam a picture of a Pontiac GTO. Based on the front end, Sam could tell it was a nineteen seventy model.

"Is that what he was driving?" Sam asked, wondering how Sienna could have gotten a picture of it.

"He still owns it," she said. "My dad and brothers helped him restore it about ten years ago." Her pause meant she had more to say on the subject. "I remember when they started tearing it apart." The cop put her phone back into her pocket before continuing. "The front right fender had a big dent in it. Pete claimed he had hit a deer."

"I guess it's too much to ask that your dad or brothers kept any of the pieces they took off the car."

"It's possible. My dad is kind of like a pack rat. No matter what it is, he always thinks that he might have a use for it one day in the future. If he still has any of the pieces, they'll be in the barn behind the house."

Sam couldn't believe her luck. In spite of everything, all of the pieces were starting to come together. If the fender was still in the barn, there was a slim chance that they could prove the mayor had struck Aaron with the car twenty-five years ago. All it would take is one drop of blood.

"We'll need a warrant," Sam said, knowing that in order to take the man down, they'd need to have rock solid evidence and a clear chain of custody.

"We should tell McMasters first."

The thought made Sam sick to her stomach. She had already caused a rift in their friendship. Telling him that they might have evidence against his friend would only make things worse. On the other hand, she knew that if she were in his position, she'd want to know.

"I'll do it."

Chapter 27

Sam could tell the sergeant wasn't happy. Although she wasn't a mind reader, she could tell that his conversation with the mayor had not gone well.

"He doesn't want to talk to me," McMasters said, shoving his hands into his pocket. "Whatever he's into is eating him up alive. I can hear it in his voice."

"I'm sorry," Sam said, wishing she had handled the situation better. While she was positive the mayor had done something wrong, she should have spoken with the sergeant before telling anyone else. If for no other reason than to give the man a heads up. She knew as well as anyone that the two of them were friends.

"It's not your fault. You were just doing your job."

When the sergeant turned to leave, Sam suggested he try to speak with his friend again. "We're not arresting anyone today." She failed to mention the new potential evidence, thinking there'd be plenty of time to discuss it after it was processed.

Sienna waited until the sergeant exited the building before she asked Sam why she had failed to bring up the car parts.

"He needs time to process," Sam replied. Deep down, she wasn't sure if she was doing the right thing or not.

"Are you going to call and get a warrant?" Sienna asked.

"Yeah. If you want to give your dad a heads up, I'll understand." While it was against department policy to even suggest such a thing, Sam no longer cared. People were getting hurt, and there would be more fallout before it was all said and done.

Without waiting for a reply, Sam walked toward the detective's wing of the building. Although it was after hours, she knew there wouldn't be any problem getting the warrant.

Dropping into her chair, she turned the computer on, then started filling out the necessary paperwork. When she got to the part that needed Sienna's statement, she hesitated. In her mind, she couldn't imagine what the mayor would do when he learned that one of his friends had offered up the potential evidence.

"My dad says that he thinks he still has the stuff, but he's not sure where it would be." The patrol cop took a seat next to Sam. "I still can't believe Pete did this."

"Maybe he didn't," Sam said, hating herself for lying to her friend. "There's a slim chance he only knows who did it."

"You think Marsha's going to care? He's kept this a secret for twenty-five years. Regardless of whether or not he killed this guy, by not telling anyone, he made himself an accessory after the fact. At best, he's going to lose his job."

Sam had been thinking the same thing. The odds of the mayor doing time if he wasn't involved were slim, but nothing would prevent his opponents from using the information against him in order to force him out of office.

Getting up so that Sienna could look over the statement, Sam began to pace around the room. Part of her wondered if she could save the mayor's job. She wouldn't have a problem with covering up his actions as long as he didn't play an active role in Aaron's death. In the grand scheme of things, his sins were no worse than her own.

When the patrol officer stated that her statement was accurate, Sam hit the enter button, then called over to the district attorney's office to let them know that she was sending over an application for a search warrant.

"I'm glad you called," the secretary said. "Marsha wants to speak with you."

A few seconds later the acting D.A. got on the line and let Sam know that the warrant for the diary had been sent. Then she reminded her that in the future, it would be best to leave the item where it was until the paperwork was in hand.

"I didn't have any choice in the matter," Sam explained. "If I hadn't agreed to take it with me, I was afraid she was going to shove it down my throat."

"How well do you know this family?"

"The mother lives across the street from me. We both sit on the homeowner's association board and see each other on a pretty regular basis."

"What about the daughter?"

"I've only seen her twice. The night she got arrested and the other day when I went to ask her questions about Aaron." Sam remembered that first encounter well. Megan and her husband had been in the middle of a fight when Sam got home. Instead of waiting for a patrol cop to show up, Sam had tried to intervene and got elbowed in the face for her effort.

"Is there any chance she killed this guy?" Marsha asked.

"I doubt it. According to the mother, the two had dated all through high school and Megan took it hard when he went missing. I just can't see her beating him to death with a baseball bat."

"Just in case, I want you to dot every I and cross every T. I don't want her lawyer to come back and say that you pinned this on her because she assaulted you a year ago."

Sam started to correct the district attorney but realized it didn't matter which one had hit her during the altercation. A good lawyer was going to state that she was trying to settle the score either way.

Changing the subject, she brought Marsha up to speed on her latest theory, then told her about the application for the search warrant.

"It sounds like you have everything in order." The acting D.A. fell silent for a few seconds. "There's no way this isn't getting out. Everyone in town's going to know about it by the time you serve the warrant."

There was no point in disagreeing. Even if Sam kept her mouth shut, she knew there were other people involved in the process that would leak the story. Some would do it out of spite because they didn't like the mayor. Others would do it because the story was too juicy to keep to themselves.

At that moment, Sam made her decision. Right or wrong, she was going to try and talk to the mayor one more time. If he was guilty, she was going to give him a chance to set the record straight before it became a matter of public record.

Chapter 28

Sam knew that she was taking a major risk by confronting the mayor again. If anyone found out that she had gone to his house to speak with him, she'd lose her job. Maybe even face charges if it turned out that he had killed Aaron Burwell.

In the end, it didn't matter to her. Sam had decided that it was more important to get to the bottom of the mystery than anything else. If she got fired, she'd just out herself and be done with it. Taking over the family business might have its downsides, but it was better than being a tool in a broken system.

Parking in front of the mayor's home, Sam considered her options. He had refused to answer the phone when she called, yet there was no doubt in her mind that he was inside the house. They guy was one step from fleeing the jurisdiction and she was determined to stop him.

As she approached the house, she heard someone turn down the sound on the television. It was a pitiful move, made by someone who had no idea what they were doing.

Instead of knocking, Sam announced that she was going to count to five and if he didn't open the door, she was going to break it down.

The threat worked. The mayor opened the door before she could reach the number three. His eyes were wild, and it looked like he was on the verge of having a nervous breakdown.

"You don't have to do this," he said, looking past her as if he expected the swat team to storm his house at any moment. "I was planning on turning myself in."

Despite her desire to hear his confession, Sam's training took over and she began to read him his rights. When she reached the part about him having the right to have an attorney present, he stopped her.

"I know my rights," he said, as he turned his back to her.

"Mayor, you need to listen to me." Sam stopped speaking as he started to walk away. Throwing caution to the wind, she followed him into the home, closing the door behind herself. "It's not the end of the world."

The statement brought the man to a halt. "How can you say that?" he asked. "My life is over. There's no starting over for me."

When the pair reached the kitchen, the mayor took a seat at the small table and began to cry. It was hard for Sam to watch. While she didn't have feelings for the man one way or the other, she felt bad for him. His entire world was about to come crashing down and there was nothing anyone could do to stop it.

Sam couldn't help but to see the similarities between herself and the mayor. Both had been living a lie for most of their lives. Her pretending to be someone she wasn't, and him hiding the fact that he was a murderer.

No secret can be kept forever, she thought. In her heart, she knew that she too would one day face her own reckoning. In spite of everything that her father had done, and was doing to protect her identity, sooner or later, the truth would come out. When that happened, she'd be just like the man sitting before her. An empty shell, praying that someone would be kind and put an end to her misery.

Taking a seat across from the man, Sam waited for him to speak. She didn't think it would take long. He was a man who needed to confess his sins.

While she waited, Sam wondered if she was making a mistake by continuing to pretend to be Sam Wright. There was nothing holding her back from taking her rightful place in her father's organization. It wasn't like she had any true friends in her current life. At best, she had a few people who might care if she lived or died.

What am I waiting for?

The longer she thought about it, the more she realized there was no answer. As much as she enjoyed being a cop, it hadn't been her lifelong dream. It was a means to an end. A way to help the family. The realization brought a sense of relief.

I won't have to pretend anymore.

For a brief moment, Sam was happy. Then the voice

in the back of her head told her that she wasn't considering the consequences that would come as a result of her telling the truth.

Sam suspected that the first thing would be the members of her department launching an investigation into her actions. Not only had she lied in order to become a cop, but she had also influenced hundreds of investigations and through her actions, put innocent people in jail. Then, there was the personal betrayal.

From the chief down, everyone she had worked with over the last five years would be devastated to learn the truth. Some might admit they were fooled, but others would claim that they knew something was wrong with her all along.

The thought made Sam realize there was no easy way out. Like the mayor, she'd be crushed when the truth was exposed. Turning her attention back to the man, she asked if he wanted something to drink.

Instead of answering her, he got up and poured them both a glass of water. Once he sat back down, he asked her what would happen now.

The correct thing would have been to tell him that it

wasn't up to her, but she knew he wasn't interested in the truth. He was looking for a life preserver. A shred of hope to keep him going while he awaited his fate.

If it had been anyone else, she would have laid the hard truth on him. Tell him that the odds of him spending the rest of his life in San Quentin were right up there with the sun rising the next day, but she wanted to take it easy on him. After all, he was friends with her mentor, and that carried a lot of weight in her book.

"I'm not going to lie and say it'll be easy, but you have a lot of friends in this town. I'm sure Marsha will take that into consideration when she decides what she wants to do about it."

The mayor shook his head. "I'm the reason she's not going to keep her job."

"What are you talking about?" Sam asked.

"We're bringing in someone else to be the new district attorney. It wasn't personal," he said, keeping his eyes on his hands. "She just doesn't have the experience."

"Okay." Sam didn't know what else to say. Thinking it would be better to move on, she asked him the one question that had to be asked. "Why did you kill him?"

In less than a second, the mayor launched himself out of the chair and backed away until he slammed into the counter on the opposite side of the room.

"I didn't kill him. He was already dead when I found him."

Chapter 29

At first, the words coming out of his mouth didn't make sense. Sam had been expecting him to confess to murdering Aaron. While she had been ready to believe it might have been an accident, she was unprepared for a complete denial.

"Calm down," she said, before leading him back to his seat.

"I didn't do it," he said, attempting to pull himself free from her grasp. "You got to believe me. He was already dead when I took his watch."

The statement caught Sam off guard. Her entire theory of the crime had just flown out the window. As her brain raced to catch up, she forced the man down into the chair.

"Start at the beginning."

For a second, she didn't think he was going to speak. He seemed to have trouble putting the words together. Then he told a tale that defied the imagination.

In the spring of two thousand, he had decided to become a drug dealer. Relying on his experience in growing grapes, he chose to cultivate marijuana. The abandoned Owens property proved to be an ideal location. Not only was the ground conducive to growing the plants, but the land was also owned by a police sergeant, so he knew that no one would stumble across his crop.

During one particular rainy day, he chose to check out the home. In one of the back bedrooms, he discovered a small trap door leading down to the crawlspace. Thinking there might be something cool hiding below the floor, he decided to take a peek.

Due to the decomposition of the body, he had no idea who it was. At the time, he assumed that Sgt. Edwards had planted the body below the house. Coupled with the fact that he was growing pot on the property, he chose to keep his mouth shut.

"What about the watch?" Sam asked, trying to wrap her head around why the guy would keep the secret for more than twenty-five years. An anonymous call from a payphone would have been sufficient.

"I thought it would be worth something." The mayor shrugged. "You've got to remember that my parents had just cut me off. That's the whole reason I started selling dope."

"What'd you do with it?"

"My plan was to sell it, but then I saw the inscription. I knew that if I did, someone would link me to the body and I'd end up doing hard time, so I kept it."

Sam wanted to reach across the table and punch the man in the mouth. Not only had he known where Aaron Burwell was for a quarter of a century, without telling anyone, but he had robbed the corpse on top of it. For the life of her, she couldn't understand why anyone would do such a thing.

"Where is the watch now?" she asked, hoping he still possessed the item.

"It's in my safe," the mayor said, getting to his feet. "I'll go get it."

"Hold on." Sam directed him to sit down. "What about the accident he had prior to being killed? Did you do that?"

"I never touched him. I swear."

"We know that you restored your GTO a few years back. Officer Larsen's father still has the grille and fender. If you ran him over, we're going to find out."

"I hit a deer in the winter of seventy-one." The mayor ran a hand over his face. "It was out by Point Reyes."

Sam didn't know what to think. While it was clear that he was telling the truth, she was at a loss as to how to explain it to everyone. As dumb as it was to steal the watch from a dead guy, then keep it a secret, it wasn't the worst crime in her opinion. When she considered her options, an idea popped into her head.

Although she would have to be careful how she presented it, Sam was sure that he'd jump at the chance to keep his secret. Taking the chance, she asked him if he had told anyone about the watch.

"I've never told a soul," he admitted. "I was too scared."

"Here's what we're going to do." Sam explained that he was going to give her the watch, then swear upon the pain of death that he would keep his mouth shut about it. In exchange for her help, he was going to owe her two favors which would be collected at some point in the future.

"Why are you doing this?" he asked.

"First off. I don't think you should go to jail for stealing a watch. Second, I like to do people favors." She could tell he didn't like that answer. "Don't worry, I'm never going to ask you to kill anyone. But if you'd rather take your chances with Marsha Dillon, I'll understand."

It didn't take the mayor long to make his decision. While he may not have liked the idea of owing the detective a favor, he had no desire to face the wrath of the acting district attorney.

"What are you going to do with the watch?" he asked.

"I'm going to use it to convict the person who killed Aaron. The less you know, the better. All you need to do is keep your mouth shut and act like everything's normal."

"What about my car? Are you going to search it to make sure that I'm telling the truth?"

"I've already gotten a warrant for the parts you left behind. As long as we don't find any human hair or blood on them, you'll be fine."

"How many people know that you got the warrant?"

"A handful," Sam admitted. "By morning, everyone in town will know about it. If anyone asks, tell them that you are cooperating with the investigation and that you have nothing to hide. I'll back up your statement as soon as we can prove you didn't hit Aaron."

"I'm not a good liar."

"No kidding. That's why I want you to stick to the truth. You are cooperating with the police and once you give me the watch, you'll have nothing to hide."

Chapter 30

Bobbi and her team were already bagging the evidence when Sam arrived at the Larsen farm. The moment the crime scene analyst saw her, she began shaking her head. A moment later, she came over and gave Sam the bad news.

"I'll run the hair we collected, but there's no way it came from a human being. Based on the length, I'd say it either came from a deer or maybe an elk."

"What about blood?"

"There was plenty," Bobbi said. "I'll test it, but again, I don't think it's human."

Sam thanked her, then walked back over to her

SUV. She didn't want anyone to overhear the conversation she was about to have.

When McMasters answered the phone, he gave Sam an earful for not telling him about the warrant. Then proceeded to tell her that things between them were going to be different from that point on.

"I understand," Sam said, knowing it would take a long time to mend the fence. "I just wanted to let you know that it looks like the mayor is off the hook. Bobbi's a hundred percent sure he wasn't the one who ran over Aaron. At least not with this GTO."

The silence stretched until the point where Sam had to check her phone to make sure the call hadn't disconnected. A moment later, the sergeant asked if she was going to make a formal statement clearing the mayor of any wrongdoing.

"I still have one more thing to check up on, but yes, I'll make sure a statement is released as soon as possible." Sam paused while she considered her next statement. "I was just doing what you taught me to do."

"I know. I just wish you would have talked to me first."

"I get it, Sarge. But if I had, someone could have accused us of playing favorites. This way, no one can say that we gave the mayor a break."

After hanging up, Sam sent a text to both Jenna and Amy. A few seconds later, her supervisor told her that they had just caught a major break in the case. The diary contained information that only the killer could have known.

Sam could feel the world dropping out from underneath her feet. It didn't make any sense. She had been positive that Megan wasn't involved.

You were also positive that the mayor had done it, she told herself.

Hitting the call button, Sam slid behind the wheel of her Ford. A moment later, Amy answered. Without bothering to say hello, she explained what she had found.

"Turns out, Aaron was cheating on her," Amy said. "Megan doesn't provide her name, but she said it was a cheerleader."

Sam remembered the mayor mentioning that Aaron had dated a girl named Jamie who had lived next door to him. She wondered if it was the same person Megan was referring to.

"It gets better." Amy read an entry that had been written less than a week before Aaron got struck by a hit and run driver. "If she's telling the truth. Aaron's stepfather was the one who ran him over. According to her, Tim had arranged for some scouts to come watch him play."

"I knew it," Sam said, thinking back to the report of Tim Creighton being arrested down in Hollister. "Does she say anything about why he lost the game?"

"No. But she talks about Aaron being upset about the scouts coming to the game. She also talks about the games being rigged." Amy paused for a few seconds, then congratulated Sam for putting all the pieces together.

"Not all of them," Sam said, thinking about the watch sitting underneath her seat. "Have you talked to Marsha yet? I'm thinking that we're going to need several search warrants and some arrest warrants."

"Don't get ahead of yourself. We still need to talk to these people before we can call it a day."

Sam was no longer listening. "What about Megan?

You said that you found something tying her to the murder."

"You mean besides the fact her boyfriend was cheating on her?"

"Yes." Sam replied, wishing she could reach through the phone and pull the answer out of the detective. "What makes you think she had anything to do with his death?"

"Two days before Aaron went missing, Megan mentions finding a small pot farm on the Owen's property. Her plan was to lure him there, then call the cops and get him arrested. We're thinking once she got him there, she confronted him about the affair."

"Then whacked him when he admitted to it," Sam said, finishing Amy's sentence. It all added up. "We'll need to talk to Megan again."

"Jenna wants us to go through the mother's house just on the off the wall chance that she kept the baseball bat or watch."

The watch. Sam reached down and picked it up. Once she planted it, they'd have everything they needed to convict Megan of Aaron's murder. Her next thought was about Christine. The woman was going to be devastated when she learned that her daughter had killed the man she claimed to love.

Sam glanced at the clock on her dashboard. It was already after nine, and she needed to speak to Carol before she called it a day. After thanking Amy for all of her hard work, she agreed to meet the detective bright and early the next morning to go over the game plan.

Now that they knew who the killer was, things were going to move fast. Their hope of course was to get a confession, but based on what they already had, they were sure the D.A. could get a conviction without one.

"It's over," Sam said to herself. Part of her wanted to go by the mayor's house and let him know that he had been cleared, but she didn't have the energy to put in the effort. She had already put in fourteen hours and still had a few more before it would be over.

Chapter 31

"So what do you need us to do?" Carol asked, picking up the watch. She turned it over and read the inscription on the back. "Such a waste," she said, putting it back in the rag that Sam had used to wrap it up.

"It is." Sam took a few seconds to wipe the fingerprints off again, even though she was sure the former prosecutor would have done it before it was passed along to either of her cousins. The woman was nothing if not thorough. "I need someone to plant this in Megan's house. She lives over in Cotati."

"What about fingerprints? Aren't the Cotati police going to wonder why the woman would have wiped it clean if she thought no one was ever going to find it?"

"I thought about that, but there's no way for me to get her to touch it."

The former assistant district attorney picked up the watch again. "Transferring prints is darn near impossible, but what about DNA? I could get one of our guys at the jail to collect some spit or blood."

It was better than nothing. Sam's idea had been limited to putting the watch into something the suspect owned. A sock or maybe a t-shirt. Feeling like they had solved the biggest problem, Sam gave the bar owner Megan's current address.

"Hold up," Carol said. "How long has she been in jail?"

"A little over a year. But her sister has been keeping an eye on the place while she's been away. I guess she wanted her to have a place to stay when she got out."

"How soon do you need this to happen?"

"If you could get it done tomorrow, that'd be perfect. I'm sure my boss is going to be itching to get the warrants now that we can prove motive and opportunity."

"Even with the warrant in hand, you're still going to

need Cotati to go along to serve it. That should buy us a day or two."

"I wouldn't count on it," Sam said, knowing how well all the area agencies worked together. "Maybe if she lived in Santa Rosa. They always have a lot on their plate."

"Let me see what I can do." Carol picked the watch up and put it in the safe. "Is there any particular place you want it to be found?"

"I don't care. Just don't make it impossible to find." Sam took a second to think. As far as she could tell, they had thought of everything. "By the way, I think I've made my decision."

Carol took her seat. "Based on the way you're acting; I have to assume that you've decided to remain a cop."

That would have been the easy choice, but Sam knew she was living on borrowed time. At some point in the near future, one of two things was going to happen. She'd either let something slip or get caught breaking the law.

When she told Carol that her decision was to start

laying the groundwork to transition from police detective to mob leader, Sam thought for sure the woman was going to have a heart attack.

"I'm so happy for you," the bar owner said, coming around the desk as fast as her feet would carry her. "Have you told your father yet?"

"No, and I'd appreciate it if you didn't say anything until I've had the chance to break the news to the family. It's going to take them a while to get used to the idea." Sam was thinking about her cousins. Paul and Chris both saw themselves taking over the family one day in the not-so-distant future.

"I won't say a word." Carol reached out and took Sam's hand. "I knew you'd come to the right decision. I'm so proud of you."

"Are you sure you're okay with this?" Sam could sense that Carol had wished she had been given the opportunity to join the family.

"In my opinion, your father should have been preparing you for this since the day you were born." She gave Sam's hand a squeeze. "I know it wasn't possible at the time, but it was clear that he was going to be in charge of the family one day. You taking over for him, should have been planned out."

Sam could understand why the former prosecutor felt that way, but at the same time, she was looking at the past as it had happened, instead of remembering how it all had unfolded. Twenty-five years ago, no one, including her father, had expected him to become the boss.

At the time of her birth, Tony was still the lowest capo in the organization. While he had been making a name for himself, there was a huge difference between being a good earner and someone capable of leading the family.

"That doesn't answer my question," Sam said, wanting to get a sense of how the woman would react to having someone so young take over the family.

"Am I okay with you taking over one day? Of course I am. I've been waiting for the day that a woman could lead a family. If anyone had asked my opinion, I'd have said that it should have happened decades ago."

"I'm not talking about some woman being in charge of some other family, I'm talking about me taking over this family. Are you okay with that?"

"Oh, I understand what you mean. You want to know if I'll be okay with taking orders from you." The bar owner didn't hesitate. "I'd be proud to pledge my loyalty to you. I only hope that you take over while I'm still young enough to be of help."

Sam wrapped her arms around the woman's neck. As they both shed tears of joy, she wondered if she had come to the right decision. There were still many things she didn't know about the business and despite her desire to be the best boss possible, she wasn't sure she had what it took to make the big decisions.

That's a problem for another day, she thought.

Chapter 32

It was nearing midnight when Sam pulled into her driveway. The adrenaline that had kept her awake was failing fast. If she didn't get into bed soon, she was afraid she'd collapse. Pushing the car door open, Sam stepped out into the cool night, wishing she owned a time machine. In the morning, she'd have to cross the street and deliver the devastating news to Christine.

Pushing the thought aside, she started toward the door when she heard a sound coming from the opposite side of the street. Cursing her luck, she glanced over her shoulder. The sight of her neighbor headed in her direction made Sam regret buying the house in the gated community. Someone was always aware of her coming and going.

"I thought I heard you drive in," Christine said, sidling up next to Sam. "It's taken everything I've got not to call you. Did you find anything in the diary?"

Sam tried to figure out a way to soften the blow, but the truth must have been written all over her face. Before she could deny it, the retired nurse broke down and started sobbing. Allowing the woman to lean against her, Sam helped her into the house.

After getting Christine settled onto the couch, Sam offered to make them each a cup of coffee. While it brewed, she considered her options. The case had just taken a major turn, and if she gave away too much information, it could compromise the investigation. In the end, she decided to tell the woman the truth without giving away too many details.

Sitting across from the aging woman, Sam explained that Megan had known certain details of the first accident, including who had run Aaron over. When pressed for details, she fell back on the standard answer every cop gave when the investigation was still in full swing.

"What about the murder?" Christine asked. "Did she kill him?"

"At this point, we're not sure," Sam answered, grateful that she didn't know. "I haven't read the diary yet, but it looks like she may have played some role in his disappearance." Sam reached across the small coffee table and patted Christine's hand. "It's possible that she was just venting and didn't have anything to do with it."

"I should have known," Christine said. "In some strange way, I think I did. When Aaron first talked about not going to college, things changed between them. He was her way out of this town. I guess when she figured out that it wasn't going to happen, she just snapped."

Sam could see the woman was trying to come to grips with the news, but at the same time trying to find some sort of justification for it.

"Don't assume anything yet. Like I said, it's possible that Megan was just venting her anger when she wrote those things in her diary."

"You're sweet, but we both know she did it." Christine wrapped her arms around herself and started rocking back and forth. "How am I going to tell my girls?"

The question had no answer. Sam knew it was just a matter of time before the news broke. Within days, everyone in town would have an opinion, and most would put the blame on Christine and her dead husband. They would think the couple had failed to raise their children the right way. The fact the retired nurse had two other children who were contributing members of society would be ignored.

"Nothing has to be done tonight," Sam said, wishing she had a better answer. "Just so you know. We're going to need to search your home for any evidence Megan may have left behind."

"I suspected as much." The woman glanced out the window at the dark homes next to the one she lived in. "I guess there's no way to do it in the middle of the night while everyone's asleep."

Sam shook her head. No matter what she wanted, Jenna had a job to do, and would have the place crawling with cops in just a matter of days. Everyone who lived in the Willowdale neighborhood would know about it. Sam suspected more than a few would demand that Christine sell her home and move away.

"I'll do what I can, but they're not going to let me be a part of that side of the investigation."

"I understand." Christine didn't seem to remember what to do with her hands. First, she tried to put them into the pockets of her robe, then tried shoving them between her knees. Neither option worked. "Thank you for telling me."

"I know this is a lot to take in, but none of us are blaming you. Megan made her own choices."

"It won't stop the others," she said, getting up off the couch. "Can you do me a favor? Can you please tell Mrs. Burwell, I'm sorry."

"I will," Sam replied. Standing up, she offered to walk Christine home, but the woman didn't want to take up any more of her time. "If you need anything, call me, okay?"

Standing in the doorway, Sam watched her friend cross the street. It looked like every ounce of energy had been zapped from the poor woman. Like a zombie, she put one foot in front of the other until she reached her home. Then without looking back, she entered the structure and turned off the lights.

A wave of guilt washed over Sam. From the very beginning, she had ignored the obvious. The number one rule in any investigation was to look at the people closest to the victim. It was that way for a reason. The spouse or significant other was often the killer. The thought led Sam back to something Carol had said about profiling.

It may not always be right, but stereotypes exist for a reason.

Shaking the thought out of her head, Sam closed the door, then one by one, shut off all the lights until the home was dark. It felt right to her that the house should match her mood.

Like her friend, Sam put one foot in front of the other until she reached her bedroom. After placing her gun and badge on the dresser, she got undressed, then slipped into the shower. While it wouldn't erase the misery she was feeling, it would save her a few minutes in the morning.

Don't think about it, Sam told herself.

In her heart, she knew that no matter how well she prepared herself, the truth was going to come out. Megan Johnson had killed Aaron Burwell. There was nothing anyone could do to change it.

Shutting off the water, Sam toweled herself off then climbed into her bed. A part of her hoped she would wake up in the morning to find that it had all been a terrible dream. Aaron Burwell would still be missing, and Christine would still have three daughters.

As the darkness embraced her, Sam knew her prayers would go unanswered. Even God couldn't rewind time or the evil out of people. The last thing she remembered was thinking that she'd make sure that Megan paid for her crimes, as well as for breaking her mother's heart.

Chapter 33

Jenna and Amy were already in the briefing room when Sam arrived. They had used the white boards to lay out the newest theory of the crime, along with the estimated timeline. From where Sam was standing, it looked like an open and shut case. Then she noticed a few question marks on the second board.

Above them was the name Tim Creighton, Aaron's stepfather. At first, Sam couldn't figure out why the name was still on the board. Then she saw some numbers scribbled next to it. Upon closer inspection, she saw how they coincided with the teen's disappearance.

"I thought we eliminated Creighton?" Sam asked, trying to dismiss what she was seeing. It was obvious that someone felt he was still a viable subject.

"Looks like we might have jumped the gun," Jenna said, pointing to some papers lying on the table. "James did more digging, and it turns out that Mr. Creighton wasn't where he said he was when Aaron went missing."

Sam wanted to argue that the diary confirmed Megan had something to do with it, but she knew that wasn't proof. As she had explained to Christine, it could have all been the overactive imagination of a teenage girl spurned by her first lover.

"We're going to bring Mr. Creighton in for an interview." The sergeant walked over to the board and drew a line connecting the property to the suspect's name. "We know he was familiar with the house, and there's no doubt that he had a motive to kill Aaron. Between the whole last name thing and Aaron's refusal to play football, Creighton had several reasons for wanting the kid dead."

Looking at the board again, Sam saw that the stepfather had everything needed to pull off the crime. The means were obvious. He was bigger and stronger than Aaron. The motive was also clear. Now that they could put him near the lake at the time of the disappearance, it gave him the opportunity to commit the act.

"How sure are we that he was in town?" Sam asked, wondering if she had made a terrible mistake by asking Carol to plant the watch at Megan's house.

"James found several people who remember seeing him that night. He's still narrowing down the timeline, but it looks like the original report was more flawed than we realized."

Of course it is, Sam thought.

They all knew that Edwards was as worthless as they came. The man took every shortcut possible when it came to police work.

Turning her attention to the other board, Sam saw her victory slipping from her grasp. Megan still had the means, motive and opportunity, but they strong compared to the stepfathers. That was until they found the watch she had planted. That alone would seal the woman's fate.

"When are we going to talk with Megan?" Sam asked.

"Lucky for us, she's not going anywhere, so we can

save her for last. I want to nail down where Creighton was on the night of the murder. According to Megan, he was also the one who ran over Aaron a few months earlier, so we need to nail that down also. I'm thinking you were right, and the two cases are tied together."

No matter how Sam spun it, she could see that her boss was right. Tim Creighton was the most viable suspect they had.

So why was I so quick to dismiss him? Sam asked herself.

When she thought about it, there was no good reason. Her original theory included him. He was the one who had the most to lose. Then she remembered the scouts the stepfather had convinced to come to town. If that wasn't enough motive to kill the boy, nothing was.

Feeling like she had made a major mistake, Sam excused herself, then headed for the bathroom. She needed to reach out to Carol and make sure that no one planted the evidence in Megan's house before she had a chance to figure out if the woman was guilty or not.

After checking to make sure she was alone, Sam slid into the last stall and dialed Carol's number. As always, the bar owner sounded as if she were half asleep.

"Have you passed along that item yet?" Sam asked.

"Paul had one of his guys pick it up last night. Is there a problem?"

Sam wasn't sure how to respond. If she admitted to making a mistake, it could make her look weak. No one wanted a leader who second guessed themselves.

"I was just checking to make sure that everything was still on schedule."

"We're good on this end. I asked the guy to put it in the bedroom. That way, it will look like she wanted to keep it close by. I wasn't able to get a sample of her DNA from the jail, but Paul's guy assured me that it wasn't a problem."

Wanting to end on a positive note, Sam thanked Carol for making the arrangements, then added that she never had any doubt that it would get done.

"It never hurts to check up on your people," Carol said. "People get lazy when they think the boss isn't paying attention."

Sam thanked her again, then hung up the phone, hoping she hadn't just sent an innocent woman to jail for the rest of her natural life. Once the cops found the watch and lifted her DNA off the surface, it would all be over but the crying.

I need to be sure, Sam thought, trying to imagine how she could delay the search of Megan's home.

Knowing Jenna, she suspected the warrant had already been applied for and would soon be in their hands. The sergeant never waited once a suspect was identified. Then she remembered her boss's statement about Megan not being able to go anywhere. As long as the woman remained in jail, there was no need to hurry.

While it wasn't much to hope for, it was all that Sam had. Leaving the bathroom, she ran back to her desk to check up on the warrant. A quick search proved that her initial thought had been correct. Jenna had applied for several search warrants.

Chapter 34

Sam wasn't surprised to see Jenna and Amy still working on Creighton's alibi. Unlike her, they liked to check their facts before they leaped to a conclusion. At least when it came to crimes not involving the mafia. Then, it didn't matter where the evidence pointed. They were all in, ignoring everything else.

Looking at the timeline again, Sam thought she saw a possible flaw in their conclusion. Pulling her notes out, she compared the two.

"According to Edwards, Aaron went missing a little before midnight. This says Creighton was still at the lake at two."

Amy nodded, then explained that they had considered that, but there was still a gap in the witness statements which would have allowed Tim time to sneak off, incapacitate or kill Aaron, then come back later and move the body."

"Was anyone able to narrow down the time of death?" Sam asked, knowing it would be impossible to give an accurate time considering all they had were bones to work with.

"Some dirt samples were sent off to the FBI lab, but we haven't gotten the results back. Right now, we assume he was killed on the night he went missing."

Nothing Sam saw disputed that assumption. No one had seen or heard from Aaron after he was reported missing. Sitting down across from Amy, she pulled the file over and looked at the notes the detective had taken during her interviews with Aaron's friends.

"What's this?" Sam asked, pointing at the page. "This guy claims he saw Aaron at the Stop & Go around five the next morning."

"He told Edwards the same thing. I'm thinking he got his days mixed up." Amy reached over and pointed at the statements given by the other people who were with Aaron the night he went missing. "They called the cops at eleven thirty. There's no way Aaron could have been at the Gas & Go five hours later. His truck had already been impounded by then."

"What if he wasn't driving?" Sam shuffled the papers around looking to see if anyone had reported seeing either Tim or Megan the next morning. When she couldn't find what she was looking for, she asked Jenna if she remembered seeing anything about the pair.

"You're right," the sergeant said, sifting through the pages sitting in front of her. "Here we go. Mrs. Arrington swore she saw Tim leaving the Greasy Spoon at six."

"Has anyone talked to her to see if she remembers anything else?"

The sergeant shook her head. "She died in two thousand three."

Amy flipped through her notebook until she found the page she was looking for. "I can put Tim in Santa Rosa at seven that morning. He got pulled over for speeding."

Getting up out of the chair, Sam paced back and

forth as she considered her options. If she could make the other two think she had come around to their way of thinking, she'd be able to delay the search of Megan's house for a while. On the other hand, if she was right about the woman, any delay would only be a waste of time.

"Do you think we have enough to get a search warrant for Tim's house?"

"Not even close," Jenna replied. "But Mrs. Burwell agreed to let us come search her property. She isn't sure whether or not he left anything there but said we're more than welcome to come look."

"I'll call Bobbi and see if she wants to go with me."

"Amy's going to the Burwell home. I want you to call Marsha and find out what we need to do to get those warrants for Megan's place."

Sam gave Jenna a thumbs up, then headed out of the room, thanking her lucky stars. Considering that Jenna had already filed for the warrants, Sam wondered what was holding them up. The only thing she could think of was that acting D.A. had concerns about the diary.

When she reached her desk, Sam called the district

attorney's office. Before transferring her to Marsha, the secretary asked if there was any truth to the rumor floating around about the mayor being involved in Aaron's murder.

"We had some questions, but the mayor cooperated and has been cleared," Sam said, knowing it wouldn't stop the rumor mill from speculating further.

The secretary thanked her, then transferred the call.

"Good morning," Marsha said. "I take it you're calling me about the warrants that Jenna filed for last night?"

"As a matter of fact, I am." Sam took it as a good sign that the acting D.A. wasn't jumping at the bit to send her off to Cotati. "Is there a problem?"

"I'm not sure I'm comfortable using the diary as probable cause for a search warrant. If we had anything else tying her to the crime, I'd be all over it. But all we have are the words of a troubled teenager written twenty-five years ago. We were already on thin ice as it was."

"But you got the warrant for the diary," Sam said, playing along. She wanted it to sound as if she were disappointed in the delay.

"She wasn't a suspect then. The rules have changed

now. At this point, I'm not sure if we can use the diary or not." The prosecutor mumbled something under her breath, then added that she was going to speak off the record with a judge she knew and would call Sam back once she had some answers.

That's perfect, Sam thought. If the judge believed they were on shaky ground, Sam could have the watch retrieved and put in a safe place until she was sure they had the right suspect.

After thanking the acting district attorney, Sam hung up and headed for the briefing room. Jenna was the type of person who wanted to hear bad news right away.

Chapter 35

"That's ridiculous," Jenna said, reaching for her phone. "She gave up any claim of privacy she had when she left the diary at her mother's house. It's been twenty-five years."

While Sam had to agree, she was willing to bet it wouldn't make any difference to a judge. "Marsha said she'll talk to a judge about it and get back to me."

"This literally makes no sense to me. She abandoned the diary." Jenna started scrolling through her contacts. When she found the one she wanted, she held up a finger to keep Sam from talking. "Marsha's not the only one with a friend on the bench."

The call lasted several minutes. In spite of how she

felt about the case, it was clear the judge thought otherwise. When Jenna hung up, she called the man every name in the book. Some of which Sam was sure didn't apply to the judge.

"I can't believe these people," Jenna said, laying her phone down. "I swear to God, the criminals have more rights than we do."

Sam wasn't about to argue with her boss. It was true. Over the last few years, the California legislature had gone out of its way to provide more and more rights to the people who broke the law. It was a wonder anyone went to jail.

"So what do you want me to do?" Sam asked, realizing the fight wasn't over.

"Go see your neighbor. See if she'll let you search Megan's old room. Maybe we can find something else to tie her to Aaron's death."

"That's just going to put us back in the same boat. No matter what we find, they're going to say it is fruit of the same poisonous tree. We need to figure out a way to sever the privacy issue."

"She hasn't lived there since ninety-nine. How can

there be a privacy issue?"

Sam pressed her lips together to keep from pointing out the obvious. Whether or not anyone liked it, Christine was Megan's mother. A parent should be able to protect their child from an illegal search and seizure.

Amy raised her hand as if they were in a school classroom. "I have an idea." She turned her attention to Sam. "You're friends with the woman who owns the house, right? And she thinks her daughter might be involved in Aaron's murder."

"Don't say it," Sam said, shaking her head. It didn't take a rocket scientist to see where Amy was heading. She was about to suggest that Sam ask Christine to throw any evidence she finds into the trash and set it out at the curb. That would eliminate any privacy concerns. "That would make us co-conspirators."

"You already said she wants justice for Aaron. If you told her that we can't use the diary because it was in the house, then hinted that if it had been thrown away…" Amy let the sentence hang.

"You're asking me to commit fraud." Sam started pacing again. "What if we're wrong? What if Megan had nothing to do with it?"

"There's only one way to find out." The detective looked over at Jenna. "How much of a grey area would it be if we hinted that her mother should throw the evidence in the trash so that we could collect it?"

"I'm with Sam on this one. It would look like we were trying to frame her daughter." Jenna walked over to the white board and ran her finger along the timeline. "We know where Megan was a few days before the murder. Let's see if we can put her at the scene of the crime."

"It's been almost twenty-five years. Any evidence she left behind is going to be long gone," Amy said. "Unless she cut herself on a nail or something, there's nothing linking her to the place."

"Except she's already admitted to being there." Jenna pointed to the copies they made of the diary. "Even if we can't use it in court, it doesn't mean we can't use it against her during an interrogation."

Sam knew her boss was clutching at straws. Even though Megan had retained a public defender didn't mean she was stupid. There was no way that she was going to admit to being at the scene of the crime.

"What makes you think she's going to talk to us?" Sam asked. "The only way we're going to get her to talk is if we offer her a deal, and I'm not ready to do that."

"Then what do you suggest we do?"

The question hung in the air like a bad smell.

"Let's forget about Megan for now," Sam said. "We'll focus on Creighton and see where that takes us."

The sergeant looked over at Amy, then nodded her head in agreement. "Okay. Amy, you chase down anyone else who was at the lake that night. Sam, you go with Bobbi and see if he left anything at his ex-wife's house."

Grabbing her notebook, Sam saluted her boss, then headed out of the room. Although she had managed to buy herself some time, she knew the reprieve wouldn't last for long. Jenna was not the kind of person to give up. Having grown up in Camden, she knew more than a few powerful people in town. At some point, she'd find someone willing to lean on a judge.

Exiting the building, Sam turned left, then walked toward the small crime lab that sat behind the station. After knocking, she opened the door and was immediately struck in the face by a horrible smell. It was like a mixture of fresh vomit and burnt hair.

"What is that smell?" she asked, covering her nose.

Bobbi looked over at her assistant who refused to meet her gaze. "Ask him."

Sam shook her head as she backed away from the door. She couldn't understand how either one of them could remain inside the building. Turning into the wind, Sam took several cleansing breaths while she waited for the crime scene analyst to join her.

"Ripe, isn't it?" Bobbi asked.

For a second, Sam thought about heaving her guts onto the woman's shoes. She thought that would be the perfect answer to the question. Pushing the thought from her mind, she asked if the analyst had time to go out to the Burwell place and look for any clues that might have been left behind.

"I'd love to, but as you can see, I'm a little busy at the moment." Bobbi leaned up against her SUV, then ran her hand over her mouth. "What are the odds that you will find anything?"

Sam had to admit they were slim.

"I'll make you a deal," Bobbi said. "I'll call Dean

and ask him to stop by on his way back from the dump. If you find anything before he gets there, call me and I'll come out."

While not ideal, Sam knew she didn't have any other choice. She thanked the analyst, then made her way back to the station. There was one other option she wanted to try before she drove to the Burwell house.

Chapter 36

Mrs. Burwell was waiting on the front porch when Sam arrived. She looked as if she had aged several years since Sam had last seen her.

"Thanks for coming," she said. "Can I get you anything?"

Sam shook her head. Right away, she could tell there was something on the woman's mind. Instead of asking what it might be, Sam tilted her head in the direction of a worn out shed sitting next to the house.

"Is there anything in there?"

"Just an old lawnmower that won't start." The woman turned her attention back to Sam. "I got a call from Christine Rodgers this morning."

Oh great. Sam cursed herself for talking to Christine about the case. Seeing the state that Mrs. Burwell was in, there was no doubt in her mind how that conversation had gone.

"She thinks that Megan might have killed my boy." The woman looked Sam in the eye. "Is that true? Did she kill Aaron?"

"I don't know," Sam answered. "We're still investigating." Feeling like she needed to change the subject, Sam asked her if she remembered where her husband was the night of Aaron's disappearance.

"He told me that he was up in Mendocino bidding on a job. At the time, I had no reason to question him about it."

Sam explained that several witnesses put him at the lake that night, and they had discovered that he had gotten a ticket in Santa Rosa the next morning.

"I knew about the ticket," she said. "He came into the house waving it around, saying how the cops up there had set up a speed trap. As to whether or not he was at the lake the night before, I can't say. If he was, I didn't see him."

"You were there?"

"Yeah. I went with a few friends of mine to watch the fireworks. We got there about seven and left right afterwards."

"Did you see Aaron and his friends?" Sam asked, wondering why her whereabouts hadn't been in the original report.

"I hadn't seen him since early that morning. He liked to get to places early, especially when there was live music playing. When he left, he said he was heading up to the lake to help the band set up. Aaron was always doing stuff like that."

Sam thought about how she wanted to ask her next question. There was no easy way to do it, but it had to be done.

"Do you think it's possible that your ex-husband hurt Aaron?"

"There's no doubt about it. Those two were like oil and water. Never got along. It didn't seem to matter what Aaron did, Tim was always ragging on him about something. Like that truck of his. Aaron spent a year fixing that thing up. He even rebuilt the engine. Yet, Tim still wouldn't let him park here in the driveway. Forced him to leave it out on the street. He claimed it leaked oil."

Sam glanced at the gravel driveway and wondered what difference it would make if the truck leaked oil or not. Then she realized it wasn't about the truck. It was Tim showing the boy that he was in charge.

"Did your ex ever strike Aaron?"

"Not after Aaron started playing football. That boy put on thirty pounds his freshmen year. After that, Tim never raised a hand to him."

"What about the night Aaron got hit by the car? Was your ex-husband home that night?"

Mrs. Burwell looked past Sam toward the road which ran in front of the house. "No he wasn't. He swore up and down he was with Bill that night."

Isn't that convenient? Sam thought. It seemed like every time Tim needed an alibi, he was with his cousin, the cop. She was about to ask a follow up question, when she noticed Mrs. Burwell reaching for the banister. The interview was over.

"Why don't we go inside?" Sam asked, opening the front door. "I'll just take a quick look around, then get out of your hair."

Once she got the woman settled into the recliner, Sam asked her if she knew of anything her ex-husband might have left behind.

"As far as I know, he took everything he owned when he left, but feel free to search wherever you like. I have nothing to hide."

Sam thanked the woman, then headed down the short hallway. The two bedrooms were separated by a bathroom which wasn't big enough for one adult, let alone three.

If it wasn't for the posters of rock bands hanging on the wall, Sam wouldn't have been able to tell the difference between the two rooms. They were both painted the same color and had the same ugly carpeting. Sam chose the main bedroom first.

As she had expected, there was nothing inside the room that indicated a man had ever lived in the home. No men's shoes tucked under the bed. No photos of the ex-hanging on the wall. It was devoid of anything masculine.

Shutting the door, Sam moved on to Aaron's boyhood room. Like Christine, Mrs. Burwell had created a time capsule in her home. Other than a thin film of dust on everything, it looked like the teenager was still living in the house.

Opening the dresser drawers, Sam noticed it was still full of clothes. The sight made her sad. Mrs. Burwell had refused to go on with her life after her son vanished.

A minute later, Sam stepped out of the room and closed the door. There was no reason to continue the search.

After thanking Mrs. Burwell for her cooperation, she sent a text to Bobbi, asking the analyst to call her assistant and tell him not to bother coming out to the Burwell house. There was nothing there.

Standing in the driveway, Sam realized that no matter what, she was going to make sure that Tim Creighton paid for how he had treated his ex-wife and stepson.

Chapter 37

Sam was halfway back to the station when she decided that she needed to visit the crime scene again. After flipping a U turn, she called dispatch to let them know where she'd be.

From the street, no one would have known the community center was the scene of a horrific murder. Driving around the main building, Sam parked as close to the old house as possible. Other than the crime scene tape, which was still covering the entrance, there were no signs that anything was out of the ordinary.

Opening the door, Sam took a few seconds to picture what the house would have looked like before the community center bought it. Although they hadn't yet remodeled the place, the stacks of boxes lining the walls were throwing her off.

"Can I help you with something?"

Sam turned around and saw an older gentleman staring at her. He had a phone in one hand and a heavy book in the other. She assumed that he was planning on using the book as a weapon should it become necessary.

Pulling her jacket to the side, she tapped the badge on her belt. "I'm Detective Sam Wright." She saw the relief wash over him. "How long have you worked here?"

"Since they first opened," the man replied. "Name's Josh Tate." He reached an arthritic hand toward her. "They told me they finished up out here."

"We are," Sam said. "I just needed to see the place one more time." Her eyes went from him to the boxes lining the wall opposite of where she was standing. "Are you guys still planning on remodeling the place?"

"I sure hope not. If you ask me, we should have torn the place down years ago. It's been nothing but trouble since we opened the door."

"How so?"

The man explained how the first few employees had found all sorts of drug paraphernalia inside the home. Then how the local teenagers would stop by and use the place for parties and other activities.

"The minute everyone found out it was no longer owned by a cop, they thought they had the right to use it however they wanted. I can't tell you how many times we had to chase the teenagers out of this place. It's a wonder none of them had stumbled across the body before now."

"How was it found?" Sam asked, already knowing the story of its discovery.

"That receptionist of ours was out here moving boxes around when she discovered the trap door leading to the crawl space. Never did say what she was looking for."

"What do you keep in there?"

"Let me show you." The man led Sam down the short hallway and into a different room than the one the body had been discovered in. "Those crime lab people moved everything in here," he said, pointing at the boxes stacked in the corner. "As you can see, most of it is over ten years old."

Although the date was written on the outside of the boxes, Sam felt compelled to look inside each of them. She knew it wasn't unusual for someone to reuse a box.

The first three contained reports and other documents related to the opening of the community center. The other boxes were filled with old flyers and pamphlets. She couldn't imagine why anyone would feel the need to keep them, let alone go looking for them a decade later. Putting the lids back onto the boxes, Sam asked the old man if the receptionist was working.

"She quit the morning after she found the body. Not that I blame her. I didn't even see it and still thought about quitting."

Sam thanked the man for the information, then headed for the exit. She needed to speak with the woman and find out why she had been inside the room that night.

What was she looking for?

When Sam reached her unmarked Ford, she texted Jenna to get the name and address of the receptionist. When the sergeant asked why she needed it, Sam explained there was no obvious reason for the woman to have been in the room on the night the body had been found.

"Hold on," Jenna said. A few seconds later, she came back onto the line and told Sam that no one had bothered to ask the receptionist what she had been looking for when she discovered the body. "How old was the stuff in there?"

"All of it is more than a decade old. It's a bunch of pamphlets and other garbage that should have been thrown away years ago."

"So why was she in there? Could she have been looking for something to steal or a place to hide something?"

"I don't know, but I'm dying to ask her," Sam replied. "I'm going to talk to the manager and see what I can learn about her. Text me her address when you find it."

For the first time in days, Sam thought they had stumbled across something useful in their investigation. While there was a slim chance that the receptionist was telling the truth, Sam didn't believe it. No one would go through ten-year-old boxes unless they had a very specific reason.

When Sam got inside, she stopped by the front desk and asked if the manager was available.

"Sure, hold on a second." The young woman tapped her keyboard a few times, then picked up the phone. "Mr. Long. There's a detective out here to see you. I'll send her right in." The woman pointed at the narrow hallway on her right. "Last door on the left."

"Let me ask you a question. Did you know the person who worked here before you?"

"Oh, I'm not the receptionist. I'm just filling in until we can find someone to replace her. As you may have heard, she quit the morning after she found the body."

"Do you have any idea why she was in the house that night?" Sam asked.

"Mr. Long sent her in there to find something."

Crap. Sam thanked the woman, then went in search of the man who had sent the receptionist into the house. With each step, she felt her new theory of the crime fading away.

Chapter 38

"Yes I did," Mr. Long said, motioning for Sam to sit down. "The remodel was set to begin at the end of the month, and I wanted the original plans we had drawn up right after we bought the place. I'd have looked for them myself, but my back's been acting up."

You lying dog, Sam thought.

The minute she saw his manicured nails, she had known why he had sent the receptionist to look for the plans instead of going to find them himself.

"Any idea why she lifted up the trap door?"

"That I can't tell you," he said, shaking his head. "I don't know what possessed her to do it. If it'd been me, I'd have never lifted it up." He paused to stare at one of the inspirational posters on the wall. "I guess in some way, it's a good thing she did. We may have never found the guy if she hadn't."

"What was the plan for the building?" Sam asked, thinking that someone would have looked in the crawlspace either way.

"Tear out some walls, lay new carpeting. That sort of thing. All we use it for is storage, so we weren't going to do anything major."

Sam felt her phone vibrate. There was no reason to look at it. Jenna was sending her the information that she had requested.

"It's a shame Katelyn quit, but if I were in her position, I might have done the same thing."

Of course you would have, Sam thought. *After you crapped your pants.*

Getting to her feet, Sam thanked the man, then handed him her business card. "I'll let you get back to what you were doing," she said, turning away from the guy.

Once she was outside, Sam called Jenna to let her know that the mystery of why the receptionist was inside the house had been solved.

"Well that's disappointing," Jenna said. "It still may not be a bad idea to talk to her again. Maybe she'll remember something new."

Although Sam had her doubts, she agreed to swing by the young woman's apartment on her way back to the station.

"How are things going there? Any luck on getting a warrant to search Megan's place?"

"I've called every judge I know. They're all scared we'll violate her privacy. As a matter of fact, two of them warned me not to try and use the diary against her should we be able to prove she killed the guy. Said they'd toss the book, and anything related to it, if the case landed on their docket."

"Sounds like they're not buying your theory that she abandoned it when she moved out of the house." Sam paused while she got into her Ford. "What about Amy? Has she had any luck chasing down anyone who might have seen Tim leave the lake?"

"I haven't heard back from her yet. Do me a favor. Swing by your neighbor's house and see if she happens to remember anything else about the days leading up to Aaron's disappearance. Maybe we'll get lucky, and she'll remember her daughter mentioning that she wanted to kill him."

"Can a mother still testify against her own child?" Sam asked.

"Don't say that too loud," Jenna replied. "We don't need to put ideas into anyone's head."

Sam laughed, then told her boss that she'd call her after she spoke to Christine.

Putting the key into the ignition, Sam took one last look at the small house sitting in the distance. Part of her wondered if they'd ever figure out who had killed Aaron. She started to reach for her seatbelt when she spotted Mr. Tate heading in her direction. The old man was moving pretty well for his age.

Figuring she'd meet him halfway, Sam slid out of the SUV and started toward him when all of a sudden, he changed direction and started toward the house. She was about to turn around when he glanced over his shoulder and waved for her to follow him.

"What's going on?" she asked, as she caught up

with him.

"I found something when I was locking up the house. Looks like it might be a necklace, but I can't be too sure. My eyes don't work like they used to. It seems like every day they get a little worse."

Keeping pace with the man, Sam wondered how Bobbi and her team could have missed something like a necklace. It seemed impossible. They were all true professionals and had searched the place from top to bottom to ensure they had recovered every shred of evidence which would later be used to link the killer to the crime.

"Over here," he said, pointing a gnarled finger at the back porch. "I came back here to make sure the door was locked when I spotted something winking at me."

Sam moved from side to side looking for anything shiny. She was beginning to think that the man had lost his mind, when the tiniest bit of light was reflected back at her. It was so small, she almost missed it.

Pulling a pair of gloves from her pocket, she got down on her hands and knees and moved toward the object. A two-inch length of chain was visible to the naked eye. Based on the color, she assumed it was gold.

"Did you disturb the dirt?" she asked.

"Just enough to see what it was," Josh replied.

Sam bit her lip to keep from cursing the old man out. After taking several photos with her phone, she called Bobbi. As tempted as she was to remove the necklace from the dirt, she didn't want to disturb the scene further, just in case that wasn't the only thing buried in the yard.

"You found what?" Bobbi asked.

"Looks like a necklace. I can see what looks like a charm, but the person who found it moved some of the dirt around to get a better look, so I can't be sure."

After mumbling several choice curse words, Bobbi stated that she was on her way and not to touch anything until she had a chance to see it for herself.

"This isn't my first rodeo," Sam replied, but the crime scene analyst had already hung up.

Chapter 39

Sam stood off to the side as she watched Bobbi and her team work. Meticulous was the word that came to mind. Instead of lifting the necklace out of the ground, they cleared a one-foot section of ground, and pulled up the grass before using what looked like a paint brush to move the topsoil away from the item.

"It doesn't look like it's been there very long," Sam said, thinking they were wasting their time.

"It's hard to tell with gold," Bobbi replied. "It doesn't corrode like other medals. If the ground hadn't been disturbed, I'd say it's been here a while, but now I'm not so sure." She looked up from what she was doing and stared at the old man standing next to Sam. "Did you use your hands or your foot to uncover it?"

"Both." The old man shrugged, then turned to Sam. "I just wanted to see what it was."

"Don't worry about it." Although he had disturbed the scene, Sam couldn't blame the man for trying to help. If it hadn't been for him discovering the necklace, they'd have never found it. "We have other techniques to determine who it belonged to and when they might have dropped it."

Sam saw Bobbi roll her eyes. She didn't blame her either. By moving the dirt, the old man had made her job harder.

A few minutes later, the crime scene tech used her fingers to remove the necklace. Holding it up, she used the paint brush to wipe away the dirt.

"You're going to want to see this," she said to Sam. Keeping her voice low, she read the inscription on the back of the locket. "I'll love you forever. Aaron."

Looking at the broken chain, Sam could imagine Aaron and Megan standing next to the old house having an argument. One or the other ripped it off the girl's neck and threw it in the dirt, where it lay undiscovered until that moment.

Now I can prove she was here, Sam thought.

While it may not be enough to convince a judge that she was guilty, there was no more doubt in Sam's mind. Megan had lured Aaron to the house and then killed him. Whether he had cheated on her no longer mattered. It was time she paid for her sins.

Sam waited until Bobbi bagged the necklace, then signed her name on the designated line. She just hoped it would be enough to get the search warrant.

"I need to call Jenna."

"Let her know that we're going to make a sweep of the yard with the metal detectors just in case we missed anything else the first time around."

Sam jotted down Josh's information in case they needed to speak with him again, then told the old man that he was free to leave.

With a sad smile on his face, he apologized again for disturbing the scene, then hobbled away in the direction of the community center.

Watching him leave, Sam couldn't help but feel sorry for the man. He hadn't intended to make their lives any harder. He was just trying to help. She made a mental note to ask the chief to give him some kind of award. Pulling her phone free, she called Jenna and updated her on what Bobbi had found.

"How certain is she that it was dropped twenty-five years ago?"

"It's too hard to tell how long it's been in the ground. The old man who found it, disturbed the scene before he reported it."

"Isn't that perfect. Have they found anything else?"

"They're going over the yard with a metal detector now," Sam said, hoping they'd find something else that they could use to prove Megan had been there around the time of the murder.

"Why didn't they do that the first time?"

Sam didn't have an answer for her boss. Not wanting to assume why the crime scene analyst had failed to search the area around the home, she asked Jenna if she thought the necklace might be enough to get a warrant.

"I have no idea," the sergeant replied. "I'll call Marsha and see what she thinks. With any luck, she'll say yes."

The same thought had crossed Sam's mind. *If it isn't, I'll have to find something that does.*

Sam knew that it wouldn't be hard for her family to come up with something that would give her a reason to obtain a search warrant. Over the years, they had framed numerous people for crimes they didn't commit. Setting up someone who had committed a crime, should be easy.

"When they're done, why don't you call it a day," Jenna said, pulling Sam from her thoughts. "You've already got thirty hours of overtime this pay period.

"Since when do you care how much overtime I have?"

"Ever since the chief told me to keep an eye on it," she replied. "Besides, it's not like Megan's going anywhere. We've still got six months to prove she killed Aaron."

"Okay," Sam said. "I'll see what I can do to hurry them along. Wanna grab a beer later?"

"No thanks."

Sam hung up, then relayed her supervisor's message to Bobbi. The analyst rolled her eyes, before telling Sam what she thought of Jenna's suggestion. While unflattering, Sam thought it was nice to hear the two were still bantering back and forth with each other. It had been a while since the analyst had joked about her boss.

"Have you two been out since she got promoted?"

"I haven't seen her in months," Bobbi replied. "We talk on the phone every so often, but it's not the same. I can tell you this. She hates being your boss. I think she'd go back to being a regular detective in a heartbeat if they would let her."

"Then why did she take the job? It's not like the chief held a gun to her head or anything."

"No, he just threatened to bring in someone from the outside. Which according to Jenna was a fate worse than death. She's been through two regime changes, and neither were good." The analyst shrugged, then went back to work.

Sam tried to think of a way to help her friend but kept coming up with the same answer. There was no way to help her.

Chapter 40

"Based on what you've told me, I can't see any judge issuing you a search warrant," Carol said. "I'm a little surprised you got one for the diary, considering it was in her mother's possession the entire time. If it had been me, I'd have erred on the side of caution and turned down your application."

"She's had almost twenty-five years to remove it from the house. It's obvious that she no longer wants it."

"Not in the eyes of the law." The former prosecutor turned her attention to the video monitors for a few seconds. Dozens of people were in the bar drinking the day away. "It could be argued that she left the diary in her mother's house because she knew it would be safe there."

Sam didn't want to argue about it anymore. What was done was done. Changing the subject to the necklace, she asked Carol why that wouldn't be enough to get a warrant.

"Do you have any proof she dropped the necklace there? Or when it was lost? Any good attorney will claim that someone placed it there in order to frame their client." The bar owner turned and looked at Sam. "Why are you so determined to keep this woman locked up?"

"She killed someone."

"Fair enough. If all you want is for this woman to spend the next couple of decades in prison, we can make that happen easily. I'll just have one of our people at the jail slip some drugs into her cell."

"I want her to go down for murder, not drugs." Sam felt herself getting frustrated. She wondered why the former assistant district attorney couldn't understand her position. Megan Johnson was a murderer and deserved to spend the rest of her miserable life behind bars.

"What difference does it make?" Carol asked. "It's not like California has the death penalty anymore.

Whether she spends twenty years in prison because she killed someone or because she was found with a few ounces of cocaine in her cell, she's still behind bars."

"It matters to me." Sam got up and paced as she considered why it was so important to her. "I need to know that I can solve a case on my own."

"You've already done that," Carol pointed out. "You know who killed this Burwell guy. Let us handle the rest."

It would have been easy for Sam to take a step back and let her family take care of it, but she couldn't bring herself to do it. She wanted to see the case through until the end. If the courts let Megan off, then she'd let her father handle it.

"What am I going to need to get a warrant?"

"To start with, you're going to have to prove that she had the means, motive and opportunity. Then, you're going to have to tie her to this guy's disappearance. Where was she when he went missing?"

"They were all at the lake together."

"How many were there?" Carol asked, jotting Aaron and Megan's name down on a sheet of paper.

"Four." Sam paused to look at her notes. "They had rented a boat and went out on the lake to watch the fireworks. Sometime afterward, the couples split up and went for a walk. A couple of hours later, Megan found the other couple and let them know that Aaron had vanished."

"Okay. So by her own account, she was alone with him right before he went missing. Did she say how they got separated?"

Sam shook her head. It was another piece of the puzzle that was missing.

"Didn't anyone interrogate this woman?"

"All they did was take her statement." Sam shrugged. "The cop who investigated is related to Aaron's stepfather. I'm guessing he thought his cousin might have been involved with his disappearance, so he did as little as possible to figure out what had happened to him."

"That doesn't make any sense. If he thought his cousin whacked this kid, why not ask him about it? At some point, he had to know that the truth was going to come out."

"Maybe he didn't ask because he was afraid of the answers he'd get." Sam looked over at the former prosecutor and could tell the woman wasn't buying it. Even she was having a hard time believing it. Nothing about the case made sense.

"Let's start over," Carol said. "Why would this cop think his cousin had anything to do with his stepson's disappearance?"

"A few months before he went missing, the stepfather arranged for some college scouts to come watch Aaron play football. For whatever reason, the kid lost the game. As a matter of fact, he threw the interception that sealed it."

"What does that have to do with anything?"

"A couple of days afterward, someone hit Aaron with their car. Since no one saw it happen, the case never got solved. Aaron spent a couple of months with a cast on his leg. Then, out of the blue, he decided that he wasn't going to play football anymore. That put an end to the stepfather's gravy train."

The former prosecutor wrote down the information, then suggested that it would be easier to tie the stepfather to the disappearance than it would be to pin it on the girlfriend. He had the motive.

"I know that," Sam said, taking a seat. "But Megan's the one who wrote about wanting to kill him in her diary. Besides, we can't put the stepfather with Aaron the night he disappeared."

"The body was found in a crawlspace, right? How did it get there?"

"If we believe Megan's diary, she lured him to the property in order to set him up. We're assuming that once they got to the house, an argument broke out and she whacked him with a baseball bat."

"Where'd she get the bat? How did they get to the property? How did she move the body after she killed him?" How did she get home afterward?" Carol began shaking her head. "This story has a lot of holes in it. Has anyone talked to this cop?"

"The night shift detective tried. He's not interested in cooperating."

"What about the stepfather?"

"Same thing. They know that as long as they keep their mouths shut, there's nothing we can do to them. We can't put either one of them at the scene or with Aaron the night he went missing."

"Then you need to figure out who was with the girlfriend when she killed him." Carol tapped the paper with her pen. "It's obvious she had help disposing of the body. The guy was a football player, right? How does a teenage girl pick up a dead body, carry it into the house, then vanish without leaving a trace?"

Chapter 41

As Sam listened to Carol explain her theory of the crime, she realized just how far she needed to go to learn how to be a good detective. For reasons she didn't want to admit, she had left too many questions unanswered. By the time the former prosecutor was done, Sam was reconsidering her entire life. It was clear that she was not cut out to be a detective.

"We've overlooked everything," Sam said, shaking her head in disgust. "We're no better than the Keystone Cops."

"I wouldn't say that," Carol replied. "You're just one part of the investigation. Have you asked your sergeant about the other parts?"

Once again, Sam had to admit that she hadn't. She knew that Jenna had Amy and James working on the case but had no idea what they were doing or why they were doing it.

I need to ask more questions, Sam told herself.

"You're just frustrated because you're used to closing the cases fast."

"I guess you're right," Sam said, before getting to her feet. When she started to pace, she wondered what her life would have been like had she not relied on her family to solve every other case she had worked on. Deep down, she knew the answer. She'd have washed out in less than a year.

"You need to keep in mind that most cases don't get solved. Real life isn't like television. To begin with, you're all overworked and underpaid. How many cases are you working on right now?"

"Twelve."

"You never see that on TV, do you? They have one case and all the clues they could want. Back when I was a prosecutor, we were lucky if thirty percent of the murder cases got solved. And half of those were circumstantial at best."

While Sam knew the woman was telling the truth, she didn't want to hear it. In her world, the cops were supposed to win, and the bad guys were supposed to go to jail.

"Will you sit down; you're driving me nuts."

"Sorry," Sam said, dropping down into the chair. "I think better when I'm on my feet."

"Let's start with the potential suspects. We have the girlfriend, the stepfather, and the cop. Considering the location and the size of the victim, we can rule out the girlfriend acting alone. You said you can't put the stepfather or the cop with the guy when he disappeared, but what were they doing after he went missing?"

"We know the stepfather was in Santa Rosa the next morning. He got pulled over for speeding. After that, he went home and complained about it. His ex-wife says he never left the house afterward."

"What about the cop? You said he may have assumed that his cousin was involved. Is there any chance he found the body and disposed of it?"

"I hadn't thought about that. It would explain why he was so eager to claim the guy ran away from home." As Sam thought about it, she remembered her conversation with Megan. "Hold on. When I told Megan that the killer might have friends who work at the prison, she all but laughed at me."

"So?"

"So that means it couldn't have been the stepfather or the cop. Both of them would know some of the guards who work at the prison."

"Maybe she wasn't worried because she knows they were involved in the murder. If they tried anything, all she has to do is point and say, 'They did it.' That gives me an idea. What if we make her think that her co-conspirators are trying to take her out?"

"Too dangerous," Sam said, thinking about the other times she had asked her family to convince someone to talk. More often than not, the person they visited ended up dying. She didn't want Megan dead. "Maybe there's another way." Sam got out of the chair and began pacing along the back wall. "Can you get me some of her blood?"

"Shouldn't be a problem," Carol said. "How much do you want?"

"A few drops should work. We found a few pieces of clothing at the scene. I'm thinking we could put some of Megan's blood on it before Bobbi sends it off to the feds."

"We don't need her blood for that. I'll just have someone I know at Quantico say they found her blood on the clothes. No one is going to question it."

"You have a…" Sam couldn't bring herself to finish the question. She didn't want to know the answer. "How long does it take the feds to run tests in a murder investigation?"

"It all depends on who was killed and where it happened. Your case involves a nobody from nowhereville, California. They won't be in any hurry to help you. But I can speed things up. We should be able to get the initial results back in a week or so."

Sam didn't want to wait a week or more for the results. She wanted to be able to drive up to the prison in the morning and arrest Megan for murder.

"What else can we do?"

"Short of putting her at the scene or finding the murder weapon with her prints on it, you're just going to have to wait."

"Even if we found the murder weapon, we'd still have the privacy issue, according to you."

"It's not my fault she left her belongings behind at her mother's house," Carol said. "There is one way around the privacy issue."

"Don't say to have her mother throw the evidence in the trash."

"That's too obvious. I was thinking of something more old school. What if the mother called the cops because someone broke into her house? In order to determine if anything was missing, they'd need to look around. Anything they found tying the daughter to the murder would be fair game."

"Except the fact that we already have the diary. It would seem a little too convenient if someone just happened to break into her home while we're struggling to figure out how to get a warrant to look around it."

"What about a fire? No one would accuse you guys of setting the fire just to get inside the house."

"I'm not burning down her house," Sam said, remembering the last time one of her cousins had burned down a house in her neighborhood. She didn't want to go through that again.

"What about a medical emergency? If she called 911, it wouldn't be unusual for a cop to show up. They could take a quick peek around the house, claiming they were looking for her purse or medication."

"No." Sam didn't want to think about what her family would do to Christine in order to get her to call 911. "I need something simple that has no chance of getting anyone hurt."

"If that's the case, then I'm all out of ideas."

Chapter 42

Sam was still thinking about her problem when she saw Jenna appear on one of the monitors. The sergeant took one look around the bar before settling into one of the booths.

"My boss is here," Sam said, pointing at the screen.

"Tell her that you were in the bathroom," Carol replied, waving for her to leave. "I'll tell the bartender to send a hamburger and beer over to your table. That way, it will look like you already ordered."

Sam thanked the former prosecutor, then slipped out of the office and turned toward the main part of the building. When she saw her boss, she smiled.

"Did you just get here?" Jenna asked.

"I was in the bathroom." Sam looked around, then waved over one of the waitresses. "My friend needs a beer."

"Right away," the woman replied. "Anything to eat?" she asked Jenna.

"I'm good."

When the young woman walked away, Sam asked Jenna if she had any updates on the case.

"We've got nothing," she said, running her fingers through her hair. "I hate to admit it, but I don't think we're going to be able to solve this one. The few people who do remember where they were that night, don't remember seeing Aaron or Megan or anyone else."

"I take it that Marsha doesn't think the necklace is enough to get a warrant."

"She's not even going to try. Says anyone could have dropped it at the community center any time over the last couple of decades."

Sam nodded, then explained that she had been giving more thought to her theory that Megan had killed Aaron in a fit of rage. Then she asked the sergeant the obvious questions to see if Jenna had considered the possibility that the teenager hadn't been alone when she killed her boyfriend.

"The only thing that I haven't been able to figure out is how she got the body into the house. Aaron was about two hundred pounds when he died. It's possible she could have dragged him into the house, but even that would have been difficult for her."

"What about the weapon?" Sam asked. "What kind of girl carries around a baseball bat?"

"The kind who plays softball. Did you look at the yearbook? There's a dozen pictures of her with a bat in her hands."

Sam didn't know what to say. When she had looked through the yearbook, she had been looking for pictures of Aaron, not Megan. It was a rookie move.

"Don't beat yourself up. We didn't find them until after you brought the diary in." Jenna fell silent as the waitress returned with their beers and Sam's hamburger. "You know what, I've changed my mind. Can you bring me one of those?" she asked, pointing at the plate.

"Sure thing. Be right back."

Sitting her notebook on the table, Sam went over what they knew. "Megan had access to a similar weapon. She was angry at Aaron for cheating on her. We know that she wanted to lure him to the property. Her necklace was found behind the house. She was the last one to see him alive. So what are we missing?"

"How she got to and from the crime scene."

"That's because we were assuming she killed him after she reported him missing." Sam flipped through her notebook until she found the page she was looking for. "She and Aaron walked off alone a little after ten. She didn't call the cops until eleven thirty. That gives her an hour and a half to drive him to the house, kill him, dump his body, then get back to the lake and report him missing."

"Good theory. How do we prove it?" Jenna asked.

"Was Bobbi able to get anything off the scraps of clothing we found?"

"She pulled some blood, but it was a match for Aaron." The sergeant drummed her fingers on the table. "If it was her, why'd she go back for the watch? Bobbi said that whoever took it, came back for it almost a year after he was murdered."

Sam had been expecting that question. It was one of the weirder aspects of the case. Now that she knew the mayor was the one who stole it, she could spin the story anyway she wanted.

"We have no idea why the killer came back. For all we know, they took the watch the night they killed him and had some other reason for returning a year later."

"Like what?" Jenna asked. "What would make you go back to the crime scene a year after you killed someone?"

"Maybe they wanted to make sure that no one had found the body?"

"Even if that were true, why move it? Bobbi says the body was moved. Something was taken off his left hand or wrist. Which brings us back to the watch."

"Let's say it was Megan. She whacks him because she thinks he cheated on her. As time passes, she realizes that she has nothing to remember him by, so she goes back and takes the watch because she knows it was important to him."

"Why wouldn't she take it the night she killed

him?"

"Would you take the time to steal a dead man's watch right after you killed him? Think about it. The murder wasn't planned. At least not according to her diary. She wanted to make it look like he was the one growing the marijuana."

"So why wait a year?"

Here we go, Sam thought. "Two reasons. First, everyone knows that a decomposing body stinks. Second, she wanted to give everyone in town time to forget about Aaron."

"If you're right, that means Megan still has the watch."

"There's no doubt about it."

Jenna leaned back to give the waitress room to sit the plate on the table. "We need to get a warrant to search her place."

Chapter 43

"I'm not saying a word until I get a deal," Megan said.

The interview was starting off just as Sam had predicted. Whether or not Jenna and Marsha wanted to admit it, there was no reason for Megan to cooperate. All she had to do was serve the remainder of her sentence, then she'd be a free woman.

"What do you want in exchange for your testimony?" Marsha asked.

"First, I want my conviction overturned." She looked at Sam. "I didn't touch her. Second, I want out of here. Today. No probation."

You wouldn't have probation if they overturned

your conviction, Sam thought.

"Anything else?" Marsha asked.

"Yeah. I want to be compensated for the time I served. I shouldn't have gotten two years. I wasn't the one who punched her in the face."

"In exchange for letting you out of here, what do we get?"

"I'll tell you who killed Aaron."

Marsha looked over at Sam and Jenna, then motioned for them to step out into the hallway. Once they were outside, she asked them if they were sure that Megan had killed Aaron.

The question was reasonable. In spite of everything, Megan was not acting like she had committed the crime.

"She's the only one who had the opportunity to do it," Jenna said. "Trust me, we've looked at this from every angle."

"What about the stepfather? Doesn't he have a history of slapping Aaron around? Where was he that night?"

"We can put him at the lake around the time Aaron went missing but can't prove he was anywhere near the house that night or any other."

Sam could see they weren't getting anywhere, so she suggested they offer Megan a deal everyone could live with. "Let's offer to get her out in exchange for letting us search her house."

"She's not getting out," Marsha replied. "At best, I might get the court to agree to keep her off probation once she's released."

"Then why are we here?" Sam asked, reconsidering her decision to keep her family from intervening. She suspected that Megan would be more willing to cooperate if she was facing a drug charge.

"I was hoping she'd agree to tell us something."

Sam rolled her eyes. She had told the acting district attorney several times that Megan wasn't going to talk unless she got a get out of jail free card in exchange.

"What about the warrant?" Jenna asked. "Isn't her refusal to cooperate enough to get one?"

"The law doesn't require her to cooperate with your investigation. You have nothing linking her to the crime. All you can do is prove that she was with the victim a couple of hours before he went missing. That's not enough for a warrant."

"What if we tell her that we can put her at the scene?"

"In spite of the evidence to the contrary, she's not as dumb as she looks."

"I wouldn't go that far," Sam said, reminding the woman of Megan's statement about wanting no probation after her record was expunged.

"I'm not saying she's the sharpest knife in the drawer, but if you accuse her of being there when Aaron got killed, her lawyer's going to shut this interview down before she has a chance to say anything."

"Then we might as well go back to Camden and come up with a new plan. Because this one isn't working."

"I've got an idea." Marsha asked Sam if she had any copies of the diary on her.

"I thought you said we couldn't use it against her," Sam said, showing her a copy of the pages on her tablet. "I didn't bring a hard copy with me."

"I'm not sure a judge will let us use it in court, but in an interview…" Marsha shrugged. "If she thinks we're trying to pin the murder on her, maybe she'll tell us who did it."

"She did it," Sam and Jenna said at the same time.

"Either way. Showing her the diary might be enough to get her talking. What I need from you two is to keep quiet. No matter what she says, I want you to act like you were expecting it. Okay?"

Sam nodded, although she knew they were giving away the only leverage they had over the woman. If she was right, Megan was going to shut down and ask to be taken back to her cell. Then they would have nothing. Not even the element of surprise.

When they re-entered the room, the public defender put a stop to the interview before anyone had a chance to say anything. While she didn't give a reason, Sam suspected she knew why the lawyer had done it. By bringing up the murder again, they had set the woman on edge.

"I only have one question," Marsha said, trying to push past the defense attorney.

"I've directed my client not to speak to any of you again. If you have more questions, you can submit them to me in writing and I'll pass them along to her. Until then, we have nothing to talk about."

"Is that true, Megan?" Marsha asked, ignoring the attorney. "Don't you want to know why we're here asking you about the night Aaron went missing?"

The woman didn't bother answering the question. She just kept her eyes on the table in front of her as if no one else in the room existed.

Seeing that they weren't going to get anywhere with the prisoner, Marsha turned and stormed out of the room.

"This was fun," Sam said to Jenna when they reached the hallway.

"Think so?" the sergeant asked. "Wait until we leave. It's a two-hour drive back to Camden."

Chapter 44

"Did she confess?" Amy asked, as they entered the briefing room.

Jenna shook her head as she plopped down into the chair at the head of the table. "All we did was waste five hours of our lives."

"I hate to say it, but I've got more bad news." Amy waited for the women to stop groaning before she explained that she had gone through the call logs for the night Aaron disappeared. "Edwards was missing for about two hours. Said his radio wasn't working."

"You've got to be kidding me," Sam said, wondering why that fact hadn't made it into the report.

"Afraid not." Amy slid a copy of the report over to

her. "Of course nothing got said about it."

Sam tried to imagine what would happen if a patrol officer tried something like that now. At best, they'd get suspended. The current chief didn't tolerate any shenanigans.

"When was the last time anyone heard from him?" Jenna asked, writing Edwards name on the white board.

"He responded to a domestic disturbance at twenty-one-forty-five hours. Fifteen minutes later, he reported that he was clear and heading back on patrol. It was a little after midnight when he called in to let dispatch know that his radio had been acting up."

"Why would a sergeant be the first one to respond to a domestic disturbance?" Sam asked, knowing that would never happen in real life.

"He wasn't an actual sergeant then," Jenna said. "Everyone just treated him like one because he was the chief's golden child."

"I take it that's why no one complained when he said his radio wasn't working."

"You got it. Back then, this was a good old boys club. If you were part of the group, you got away with murder. If not, you kept your mouth shut and your head down."

Although Sam had heard the story many times, she couldn't imagine why the city had allowed them to get away with it. Then she realized that over the last two decades, society itself had changed. Back then, the cops were still the good guys, so they got away with more, like protecting their own. Part of her wished she had worked during those days.

"Do you think we should try to interview him again?"

"It wouldn't do any good. If he had anything to do with Aaron's murder, he'll never admit to it. He knows how the system works. As long as he doesn't talk, he's safe."

Sam was tired of playing the game. It was time to ask her family to get involved. The first thing she needed was to get some leverage against Megan. If that meant putting drugs into her cell, so be it. Then she'd have them go and have a long talk with Tim Creighton and Bill Edwards. Whether they were involved or not, didn't matter. Both men needed to be taught a lesson.

"Hey," Jenna said, tapping Sam on the arm. "Are you listening?"

"What?"

"I said we should call in the feds and ask them for help. Maybe they can help us get a warrant to search Megan's house."

While Sam wanted to disagree, she knew they were out of options. If something didn't break soon, they'd be forced to drop the case and start working on something else. That was the thing about police work. There were always more cases to work.

"I might know someone," she said, trying to remember if Carol had mentioned the name of the federal agent who specialized in cold cases.

"As much as I like your boyfriend, this isn't an organized crime case. I doubt he'll be able to help us with this one."

"You're hilarious," Sam said, as she rolled her eyes.

"I heard she dumped him and was going out with Susan again." Amy turned to Sam and grinned. "I'm not saying that I blame you. Susan is hot."

"Are you done?" Sam didn't mind the good-natured

ribbing, but she was getting a little sick of hearing about how she had a thing for the premiere defense attorney. "As I was saying. There's a woman who specializes in cold cases. I think she's a profiler or used to be one."

"If you think she can help, give her a call. I'll let the lieutenant know and he can file the paperwork to bring her in," Jenna said, as she scooped up the files lying on the table.

"I've got a question," Amy said, raising her hand. "This profiler you know. Is she cute?"

"Knock it off," Jenna said, throwing a magic marker at the detective. "Who Sam sleeps with isn't any of our business."

"Sounds like someone's jealous." Amy held up her hands when Jenna raised an eraser. "Okay, I'm done. No more jokes about Sam's love life or lack thereof."

Sam rolled her eyes again, then excused herself to make a phone call. Bypassing the bullpen, she went outside and called Carol. The bar owner was happy to hear that Sam had agreed to call in a specialist.

"You swear she doesn't work for the family?" Sam asked.

"Not that I know of," Carol replied. "Even if she did, what difference would it make? You want to put this woman away, right? Then do what you gotta do."

"Text me her name and number."

"I'll do better than that. I'll have her give you a call. In the meantime, Chris wants to talk to you. He says you didn't solve that gambling problem."

"I talked to the mayor. He's not putting the game back together."

"I'm not getting in the middle of it. Chris said he'll be at your house when you get off work. You two can work it out yourselves, I'm staying out of it."

Great, Sam thought. *That's just what I need.*

Hanging up, Sam dropped the phone into her pocket and walked back to the meeting room to update the others.

Chapter 45

It was after seven by the time Sam managed to get out of the station. It had been a long day and she was looking forward to going home and having a stiff drink. That's when she remembered her cousin would be there waiting for her.

For a minute, she thought about turning around and heading back to work. It wasn't like she didn't have plenty to do. Despite their best efforts, they were still no closer to getting a search warrant than they had been the day before.

The acting D.A. kept telling them that they needed something else. The one clue which would link Megan to the murder. One that no one could dispute.

All the way home, Sam thought about what it would take. She was afraid that if the diary didn't do it, nothing would. They had no murder weapon. No fingerprints. Nothing tying her to the location at all. Other than her own musings about wanting to lure him to the home in order to set him up, they were stumped.

With the lights of the city fading in her rearview mirror, Sam considered her options. The easiest would be to get her family to frame Megan for some other crime, like drugs. Once she was facing a few decades in prison, she'd be more willing to work out a deal. Another option would be to have her killed. While not ideal, it would ensure that justice had been served.

Stop it, Sam thought. *I'm not having her killed.*

It amazed her how easily the thought had slipped into her mind. Since learning she'd be able to join the family business, the idea of having people murdered was always there. A simple solution to all of her problems.

This is how people end up in jail.

Sam had seen it a hundred times. Once a criminal got away with their crime, they got hooked on the rush it gave them. Next thing they knew, they needed it. And like any addiction, the act of breaking the law fed the desire to break more laws.

Turning off the main road, Sam shook the thought out of her head. She told herself that she needed to tamper the desire. A lesson her father had taught her when she was young.

When she looked back on that day, she understood why her father had taken the time to explain why she couldn't do as she pleased whenever the notion occurred to her.

"That's what separates the thugs from the true criminals," he had said.

Tony had always considered himself a true criminal. In his opinion, there was an art to it. Thugs on the other hand, took advantage of a situation with no thought given to the consequences. If they saw an easy mark, they acted. It's why most of them got caught.

If she were going to lead the Bongino family, she needed to weigh all of her options before making a decision. Then make sure that nothing she did could come back to haunt her. It was the number one reason why her father had never seen the inside of a jail cell. He was always one step ahead of the people who wanted to destroy him.

Slowing down at the gate, Sam realized she still had a long way to go before she'd be able to fill her father's shoes. Unlike her, he never allowed his emotions to dictate his actions. The more upset he got, the more complex his plans became.

"I can do that," Sam told herself.

Although the sun had long since dropped below the horizon, Sam noticed several of her neighbors walking along the quiet streets. It was quite the change from when she had first moved into the Willowdale neighborhood. The previous homeowner's association board discouraged such activity, preferring people to stay inside their homes after dark. They believed being out after the sun went down would lead to crime.

Striking the unwritten rule was one of the first things she suggested after taking her position on the board. As a cop, Sam knew that residents walking through the neighborhood had the opposite effect on crime. Not only did people get to know their neighbors and their habits, but they were also able to spot things when they were out of place. Within weeks, it seemed like everyone had taken up walking as their new hobby.

Sam took a few seconds to enjoy the sight. By any definition, the Willowdale neighborhood had become a community again. People were no longer afraid to meet their neighbors. The fences which had once walled them in, were now meeting places.

We did good, she thought.

At the new dog park, Sam turned right. While the small piece of land was still a contentious issue for some, she knew that it would all work out in the end. People needed to have a place to hang out. Somewhere where they didn't need to worry about how they looked. A gathering spot where they could meet new people and speak with old friends.

The thought brought a smile to her face. Regardless of the few who complained, Sam knew they had brought a positive change to the neighborhood.

Parking in front of her home, Sam stared at the front door, wondering what her neighbors thought about seeing the lights on inside her house while she was away.

Part of her was a little surprised that one or more of them hadn't called the cops.

Sam guessed it had something to do with how safe they felt. When you no longer feared becoming a victim, it was easier to overlook the subtle changes happening all around you. As she got out of her unmarked Ford, Sam made a mental note to speak to the people living around within sight of her home. If for no other reason than to let them know that on occasion one of her friends might stop in while she was at work.

The first thing Sam noticed when she walked through the door was the smell. Whatever Chris had brought with him, smelled like it was made from vinegar. It overpowered the sweet fragrance she was used to, when entering her home.

"It's about time," he said, peeking around the corner at her. "I brought dinner."

"What is it?"

"Barbecue spare ribs and something called burnt ends." Chris held up a bite-sized piece of meat. "You've got to try this," he said, shoving the charred morsel into her mouth.

Although it didn't look appetizing, Sam was amazed by the explosion of flavor. It was as if her mouth had died and gone to Heaven. "Oh my God, that's good," she said, reaching for another piece.

"I know, right? I got it at this little place over in Northmont, called the Pig and Poke."

Chapter 46

As they dined on the barbecued meat, Chris explained why he had gone to Northmont.

The small town was considered by most to be a closed community. Outlandish rumors kept most bay area residents from visiting the place. The one and only time Sam had gone there, she had felt like an outsider. While the people were nice enough, none went out of their way to make her feel welcome. That's why she was so shocked her cousin was thinking about doing business there.

"I wouldn't have considered it; except they're throwing a ton of money at the project." Chris paused to lick the barbecue sauce from his fingers. "The restaurant is about a mile and a half from the Heartstone resort."

"What'd my dad say about it?" Sam asked, knowing her father had to sign off on every job Chris took.

"I haven't told him yet." The gangster reached over and snatched one of the burnt ends off Sam's plate. "I'll talk to him this weekend. Speaking of which, are you coming down?"

Sam shrugged. The decision wasn't hers to make. While she wasn't scheduled to work, their murder investigation took precedence over everything else. She'd be expected to put in any amount of hours necessary to close the case.

"Aren't you off this weekend?" he asked.

"I'm supposed to be, but we're still trying to figure out how to get a search warrant. If we can't get inside Megan's house, we're all going to be working this weekend."

"This wouldn't have been a problem if you'd have let us whack her last year when she went after you. I don't know what you were thinking."

"For one thing, she didn't do anything to me. Besides, I can't have you guys killing everyone who looks at me the wrong way."

"Sure you can. You're a Carlucci. We can kill anyone we want."

While Chris made it sound like a joke, Sam knew that he believed it. The family had killed more than a thousand people over the last thirty-five years. Most at the behest of her father. The man did not tolerate disloyalty or disrespect.

The only reason Megan hadn't been killed was because Sam had begged her father not to take his anger out on the woman. If it had been left up to Tony Carlucci, everyone who had been on the property the night Sam was assaulted would have paid the ultimate price, not just Tyler.

Needing to change the subject, Sam asked why he was there. She knew that if she didn't, they'd talk about killing people all night long.

"I need you to figure out who's behind this card game."

"You told me the mayor was behind it." Sam got up from the table and began to pace. She couldn't remember the last time a member of her family had been wrong about something. Unlike her, they never leaped to any conclusion without knowing all the facts. "Are you sure your information is up to date?"

The mobster looked at her as if she had just bumped her head on something. "Someone we know got an invitation to the inaugural game."

"When is it?"

"August twenty-fifth. That gives you a couple of weeks to find out who's putting these games together and make them stop. If not, I have to take care of it."

"Can't you hack their email or something?" Sam came to a screeching halt when her cousin shook his head. If they couldn't figure out who was behind the game, that only left two possibilities. Either the party behind the games was going old school, or the Bongino family was being set up. She was betting on the latter. "Tell me about the guy who got the invitation."

Chris ran through the details while Sam began building a profile. Although the man wasn't connected to the family, he was considered a wise guy. Someone her cousins did business with on occasion because he could be trusted. To a point. How he had gotten invited to the game remained a mystery.

"Is he on the casino's high roller list?" Sam asked. She knew that her cousin Paul often put friends of the family on the high roller list so they could launder money through the casino without drawing too much attention to themselves.

"As far as we know, the man has never gambled in his life." Chris glanced down at his empty plate with longing in his eyes. "I can't get over how good this was."

"I need you to focus," Sam said, picking up his plate and carrying it over to the sink. "I didn't ask if the man was a gambler. I asked if he was on the high roller list."

"No, he's not. Your father hasn't made up his mind about this guy yet. We've let him do one or two things, but nothing that can be traced back to us. That's why we need to know who's organizing these games. Paul is starting to think it might be that fed you've been hanging around with."

Sam felt the contents of her stomach turn sour. If Gary was behind the illegal card game, there'd be nothing she could do to prevent him from being chopped up and fed to the sea lions. Her father might put up with the feds investigating him, but he'd never tolerate one of them trying to set him up.

"Is there any way you can put me in a room with this wise guy?"

"That's not a good idea. If he's telling the truth and his name got put on this list by accident, we don't need him knowing that you're associated with us. That could lead to an uncomfortable situation."

"What if I brought him in on some bogus charge and questioned him about the game? I could say his name came up in the course of our investigation."

"I don't like that either. If the people you work with find out this illegal gambling operation is up and running again, they might want to stick their noses in it. That wouldn't be good for anybody. Capisci?"

"So how am I supposed to find out who's running this thing?"

"Ask the feds."

Chapter 47

For the tenth time, Sam sat her phone down and walked away from it. Every fiber of her being was telling her not to call Gary. If her cousin was correct, Special Agent in Charge, Gary White was the person responsible for re-organizing the illegal card game. As the head of the organized crime unit in San Francisco, Gary was the only one who could make that call.

It can't be him, Sam told herself.

A few months earlier, he had explained how the feds no longer cared about the mafia. They were more worried about terrorists, both in and out of the country. As far as he was concerned, the mob was dead. A shadow of what they used to be.

"Then why are you afraid to pick up the phone and

find out?" Sam asked herself.

Staring out the window at the darkness, she knew the answer. If Gary issued the order to start the game up again, he was a dead man. Her father would not hesitate to have him killed. If for no other reason, because he'd want to send a message to the feds that he could get to anyone at any time.

Cursing herself for caring, Sam spun around and marched back into the kitchen. After pouring herself a glass of scotch, she picked up the phone and scrolled through the contacts until she saw his name. It had been several weeks since they had last spoken.

Here goes nothing, she thought, tapping the connect icon.

A groggy voice answered the phone. Sam paused while she thought about what to say. None of the words she had rehearsed sounded right.

"Hi," she said. "Were you sleeping?"

"It's three thirty in the morning, what do you think?" he replied. "Is everything okay?"

There it is. I have to tell him why I'm calling.

Sam took a deep breath, then told him that she had

stumbled across some information and thought he'd like to know about it.

"What kind of information?" he asked, sounding wide awake.

"Remember that illegal gambling ring I took down a while back? The one our D.A. was running? Well I heard that someone was trying to get it up and running again."

"Okay, so what's that got to do with me?"

The coldness in his voice told Sam that their relationship had changed. It was clear that he was no longer smitten with her.

"I was told that you were the one who authorized it." Sam waited for him to reply. "I guess they were right. Can you at least tell me why?"

"Sorry. I'm not authorized to talk about any sting operation we may or may not be running at this time. What I can tell you is that if we were conducting any kind of operation in the bay area, it won't have any effect on local law enforcement."

"I see. So it's my imagination that people are coming to me warning me that some criminals are organizing an illegal card game in my jurisdiction."

"Who told you about it?"

Sam felt herself shaking her head. "I'm sorry. I'm not at liberty to discuss an ongoing investigation. I will tell you this though. If that card game you're planning on having at the Veterans Hall on the twenty-fifth happens, I'm going to arrest everyone. Then I'm going to make sure that I send a copy of all the mugshots to every news station in the bay area. Including anyone who claims they work for the federal government."

"Interfering in a federal investigation has steep consequences. I'd suggest that if a card game happens to take place on the twenty-fifth, you stay away from it."

"Is that a threat, Special Agent White?"

"Just a friendly warning," he replied. "I'd hate to see you lose your job over something as simple as a card game."

"I'll take it under consideration." Sam was fuming. She couldn't believe his audacity. "In the meantime, I'd look for another location if I were you. It'd be a crying shame if someone dropped a dime and alerted the media that there was going to be a major event happening at the

Veterans Hall on the twenty-fifth."

"You wouldn't dare."

"I'm sorry, Did I forget to mention that I've already sent emails to every news organization in the bay area? You'll have to forgive me. I've been drinking."

Sam pressed the end button before he had a chance to reply. While not ideal, by sending the emails to the local news outlets, she may have just saved Gary's life. There'd be a price to pay when her chief found out, but she figured it was worth it.

Dropping the phone into her purse, Sam strolled down the short hallway, then slipped beneath the silk sheets covering her king size bed. Any messages left by the federal agent could be listened to in the morning.

Rolling onto her side, Sam set the clock for six, then cursed herself for not calling Gary right after Chris left the house. If she had taken his advice, she'd have been asleep hours ago.

Off in the distance, she heard a slight vibration. It would be Gary, calling to beg her to stop interfering in his investigation before it was too late.

Chapter 48

"Can you tell me why there's a half dozen federal agents sitting in my briefing room?" the chief asked. "They say they're here to talk to you."

Sam slid a dollar bill into the soda machine. "They're here to intimidate me." She pushed the button, then bent over to grab the cold Pepsi.

"Why would the feds want to intimidate you? Please tell me that you're not interfering in one of their investigations again."

"It wasn't my fault, Chief." Sam paused to offer him the soda. When he shook his head, she took a seat at the table. "The other day I found out that someone was trying to start up Justin's old card game. I thought it was our local mobsters doing it, so I looked into it a little bit."

"And?"

"When I couldn't trace it back to the mob, I thought the best thing to do was spread the word that we knew about it. This way, no one gets hurt."

"Back up. Are you telling me that the feds are organizing an illegal card game in Camden?"

"Yep. It was going to happen on the twenty-fifth at the Veterans Hall." Sam took a long drink while she considered her next statement. "If I had known the feds were the ones who were putting the game on, I'd have stayed out of it."

"So how'd they find out you were the one spreading the news about the game?"

"I called SAC White last night and told him about it. I'd already put the word out that we were investigating, so I figured it wouldn't hurt to tell the feds."

"Did you inform Sgt. Richards about your investigation?"

Sam thought about lying. The odds were in her favor that Jenna wouldn't remember whether or not she had told her about the illegal card game, but she didn't want to take the chance. It was easier to beg for forgiveness.

"We were already knee deep into the Burwell case when I heard about it. I was planning on telling Jenna, but then we got sidetracked with the whole diary thing."

"You've got to stop interfering in their investigations. Sooner or later, SAC White is going to get sick of you sticking your nose where it doesn't belong and have you brought up on charges."

"He's the one who didn't let us know that they were operating in our jurisdiction. One phone call would have prevented this entire situation. Maybe you should ask him why he felt it was okay to come to Camden and set up an illegal card game."

"I plan on asking him about it. Right after we finish talking about why you feel the need to keep interfering in their investigations."

Sam rolled her eyes before she had a chance to stop herself. She was tired of explaining her actions to people who bent over every time a federal agent walked through the door. Despite the few good things they had done, in her opinion, they were still more trouble than they were worth.

Knowing that her boss wouldn't leave until she explained herself, Sam laid it all out for him. If the feds wanted her to stay out of the way, they'd need to share more information on what they were doing and why they were doing it.

"It doesn't work like that," the chief said, running a hand over his face. "They don't report to us."

"Let's say I didn't do anything when I found out they were planning to start up this card game again. How many people would have ended up like Justin, lying in a pool of their own blood, with several bullet wounds in their chest?"

"I think we both know that was an isolated event."

"It wouldn't be if we let another illegal gambling operation start running games here. You know as well as I do, that desperate people do desperate things, and nothing makes people more desperate than losing all of their money."

"Did you bother to ask SAC White why they were setting up this card game?"

"I didn't know they were the ones setting it up until after the fact. All SAC White had to do was pick up the phone and let us know about the card game, and I'd have stayed out of it. But no, he decided to act like a fed and do it without telling anyone. He's lucky I put the word out on the street instead of waiting until the twenty-fifth and bust everyone."

"I'm not defending what SAC White did, but…"

"Then don't," Sam said, cutting her boss off. "I'm not the one who tried to set up an illegal card game. What they did was wrong and dangerous. Instead of standing here blaming me for putting a stop to it, you should be in there demanding to know why they were endangering the citizens of your town."

"You're being a little over dramatic."

"Tell that to Mrs. Macat. Brad shot Justin because he had lost all of his money in that card game. Maybe you don't care about that, but I do. I wasn't about to sit on my hands while another illegal gambling operation set up shop in my city. Not when all I had to do was put the word out on the street that we were watching."

Sam could tell that her last statement had reached the chief. His eyes had softened, and he no longer looked like he wanted to punch her in the face. In spite of their difference of opinion, she respected the man, and knew that underneath all of his blustering, he was a good cop. He didn't like what the feds were trying to do any more than she did. She just needed to remind him of that.

"Okay, get back to work, I'll take care of SAC White."

"Thanks, Chief." Sam was already out of the breakroom when another thought hit her. Turning back, she apologized for getting his day off to a bad start.

"The minute my assistant told me the feds were here, I knew it was because of you. There's no denying you're the best detective I've ever heard of, but at the same time, you're the biggest pain in the butt I've ever met."

"Love you too, Chief," Sam said, giving her boss a salute.

Chapter 49

"Should I get you a box, so you can pack up your crap?" Amy asked, when Sam entered the detective's wing of the building.

"You're hilarious. Have you ever thought about doing stand-up?" Sam glanced over at Jenna's office. "Who is she talking to?"

"Judge Bryan."

Sam took a seat at her desk wondering why her supervisor would be speaking with the toughest judge in the county. The man was as no nonsense as they came. If you didn't have every I dotted and T crossed when you entered his courtroom, he'd make it his personal mission in life to make you pay for it.

"She's talking to him about our case," Amy said, as if she had read Sam's mind. "It's a long shot, but if she can get him to sign off on the warrant, no one is going to question it."

Impossible, Sam thought.

According to Judge Bryan, there was no grey area when it came to the law. You were either on the side of the angels or you weren't. Based on what they had, Sam believed her boss was wasting her time. She might as well tell him that a psychic told them that Megan was the killer.

"I saw your boyfriend come in earlier. Wanna talk about it?"

"There's nothing to talk about. He tried to go behind our back and set up an illegal card game." Sam reached over and hit the power button on her computer. "I shut it down before he had the chance to get it up and running."

"What are you talking about? I didn't hear anything about any card game."

"One of my snitches called me the other day to let me know that he had gotten an invitation to play in a card game. He was worried the Carlucci brothers might be behind it."

"They weren't?"

"Nope. It turns out Gary thought it was a good idea to set up a game here. I can't imagine what was going through his mind. He knows what happened to Justin."

"Did you ask him about it?"

"After I told everyone we knew about the game."

Amy mumbled several curse words before asking Sam if she had lost her mind. Like the chief, she was worried that the feds might charge her with interfering in their investigation.

"If they were worried about their investigation, they should have told us they were conducting one. It's not my fault they can't keep a secret."

"But still." Amy let out a long sigh. "How did you find out they were the ones setting the game up?"

Sam got up and walked over to Amy's desk. She didn't want anyone to overhear what she was about to say. Leaning in close, she told the detective about her conversation with the mayor, making it sound like he was the snitch.

"Holy crap! Do you think they were trying to set

him up? Wait, he wasn't involved when Justin was running it, right?"

"No. But he has a bit of a gambling habit. He's trying to get help for it, but you know how addiction works. Sometimes he slips up."

"No wonder you didn't say anything about it." The detective shook her head in amazement. "I would have never suspected that Pete Davidson was a gambler. The man has no poker face."

"Tell me about it," Sam said as she stood up. "I'm just glad he's trying to get help. The last thing we need is for him to get caught up in some sting operation."

"But if he's breaking the law…" Amy didn't finish her statement. "I'm not saying he needs to go to jail or anything, but… He's not using city funds is he?"

"Never," Sam replied. "I would have never agreed to help him if he had."

"So what are the feds going to do now that you've ruined their operation? Are they going to move it somewhere else or scrap the idea all together?"

"Don't know. Don't care."

"I don't buy it," Amy said. "I can tell you're upset

about it. So why do you think he didn't tell you about it?"

Sam didn't have an answer for her. The same question had been plaguing her for hours. If the plan had been hatched a few weeks earlier, she'd have bet her life that Gary would have told her about it. Things had changed after she stood him up.

Good riddance, she thought.

The idea of her getting involved with a federal agent was ludicrous. Impossible from the start. Even if he did work for her father, it wouldn't have changed anything. Gary's loyalty was to the federal government. Sooner or later, that would have proved too difficult for their relationship.

Three quick taps tore Sam away from her thoughts. Knowing it was a signal, Sam first glanced up at Jenna's door, then over her shoulder. Gary looked mad enough to bite through nails.

"This isn't over," he said, trying his best to intimidate her. "You've cost us thousands of dollars and hundreds of man hours."

"Cry me a river. You're the one who didn't pick up

the phone and tell anyone what you were planning to do. So as far as I'm concerned, this is all your fault." Sam could see the shocked look on Amy's face out of the corner of her eye. "If you're done whining, I've got work to do."

"We're not going to forget this, Detective Wright."

"Neither will I, Special Agent White." Sam got to her feet and tried to make herself look as big as possible. "Don't ever threaten me again."

The agent opened his mouth to say something, then thought better of it. He tipped his head at Sam, then toward Amy before leaving the room.

"Holy crap," Amy said, staring at Sam. "You just put the fear of God into that man."

Both women turned when Jenna's door opened. The judge came out, then turned back to shake Jenna's hand. "You'll have my answer by the end of the day."

Chapter 50

Sitting on the edge of Sam's desk, Jenna explained the judge's concerns about issuing a search warrant for Megan's property.

"He said that if we had come across her diary under any other circumstances, he'd issue the warrant in a heartbeat. But because it was found at her mother's house, he's inclined to believe it falls under the right to privacy."

"Which isn't an actual right," Amy said, pointing out the Constitution had no such clause. The Supreme Court had made it up in order to protect one of their rulings.

"Be that as it may, he's concerned that if he issues the warrant, any charges we bring against her could be tossed by the appellate division."

"Did you mention that the diary was in her mother's house for more than twenty years?" Sam asked, thinking the whole subject was ridiculous. In her mind, Megan had abandoned the diary the moment she moved out.

"I did," Jenna said. "While he agrees it's odd, he's still tempted to err on the side of caution. As you know, his decisions are rock solid. I can't think of a single one of his cases that have been overturned on appeal."

It was true. Judge Bryan was a legend. Every law school in the country referred back to his cases when they wanted to demonstrate how the law should be applied. Some academics had him on their short list for the next open seat on the Supreme Court.

"So why is he willing to consider our application?" Sam asked.

"Three reasons. One, she was the last person to see our vic alive. Two, her propensity for violence. Three, the fact she's sitting in prison for assaulting a police officer is enough reason to make him believe she's capable of murder. Then there's the diary itself. Her plan to lure Aaron to the property proves she was willing to cause him harm."

"What about the necklace?"

"He's not considering it. There's no way to prove how it got there or how long it's been there. As far as he's concerned, someone could have planted it there in order to frame her for the murder."

While Sam could agree with his logic, she still wasn't ready to dismiss it. The necklace proved she had been on the property. Whether or not Megan dropped it on the night of the murder was irrelevant.

"What are we going to do if he doesn't give us the warrant?" Amy asked. "If he throws out the diary, we have nothing linking her to the murder."

"As much as I hate to say it, if he says no, we're going to have to move this case to the cold files and start on something else. We're backed up as it is."

They knew their boss was right. Both had a dozen or more cases waiting for them, and more were coming in each day. Sam glanced over at Amy hoping she could read her mind. If the detective felt like they were spinning their wheels, she'd give up on the case in a New York minute.

"Then we have what, eight hours?" Amy asked. "I'll head out and beat the bushes again."

"Me too," Sam said, reaching for her purse. She planned on speaking with Christine again. If anyone knew where Megan might have hidden the murder weapon, it would be her mother.

When Sam walked out of the room, her eyes landed on Sienna. Although the patrol cop was dressed in street clothes, it was clear that she was still working.

"Why are you still here?" Sam asked, looking around the room to see if there was an obvious reason for the officer to be in the building after her shift.

"You haven't heard the news? The chief's promoting me to sergeant today. I'm taking over for McMasters."

Sam wasn't sure if she should congratulate the patrol officer or ask God to have mercy on her soul. The promotion would come with longer hours and a ton of extra paperwork.

"It's what I wanted," Sienna said. "The chief gave me a choice of taking McMasters spot or moving over to the detective's division. I chose to stick with what I know."

"I can't say I blame you. If I had to do it all over again, I think I'd have stayed in patrol. Less downtime and paperwork."

"I'm just glad he gave me the choice. This way, I can't blame anyone else if I fall flat on my face."

"Oh please, you're the best cop in this department." Sam wrapped her arms around her friend and squeezed. "Are you staying on the midnight shift?"

"I wasn't given the choice. McMasters said if I asked for another shift, he'd come back and bust me back down to patrol."

"That sounds about right." Sam glanced at the door. It was time to go. "I gotta run. Let's meet at the Last Call later. I'll buy you a drink."

"You can buy me two."

Sam gave her one more hug, then walked out of the building. After calling dispatch to let them know where she was heading, Sam slipped her Explorer into gear and proceeded to drive west. With any luck, she'd get some answers and be back at the station before the judge had a chance to make his decision.

Chapter 51

When Sam saw the look in Christine's eyes, she could tell that something was wrong. It looked as if the woman had lost the will to go on. Before Sam could ask what was wrong, the retired nurse invited her into the home and suggested they go into the kitchen.

Four more diaries were laid out on the small table. Christine picked up the one closest to her and handed it to Sam, explaining that it contained entries dated right after Aaron had vanished.

In spite of everything, Sam couldn't resist looking at the first page. The first entry was written on the morning of July fifth, less than eight hours after Megan had reported Aaron missing. In it, she complained about the responding officers and their lack of urgency.

It wasn't until the third entry that Sam noted the reason for Megan's anger. The girl didn't appear to be concerned for his wellbeing at all. It was as if she knew what had happened to him. Every mention of his name was in the past tense. With alarm bells going off in her head, Sam asked Christine where the diaries had been found.

"Someone from the prison called me last night." The retired nurse couldn't bring herself to look Sam in the eye. "They said Megan had asked them to call. She was worried that you all were going to find them."

"Back up," Sam said, pulling her notebook from her pocket. After activating her body camera, she asked Christine to start at the beginning.

"A little before nine, someone called me and told me that Megan had asked them to get in touch with me. They said there were four diaries hidden in the air conditioning vent in her room. She wanted me to get them out and destroy them before the police found them."

"Did this person identify themselves?"

"No," Christine answered. "I swear I must have asked them a dozen times. They kept telling me over and over again that if I didn't burn the diaries my daughter would spend the rest of her life in jail." Christine picked up the first diary again, turning it over in her hands. "I had no idea they were still in the house."

Although Sam had a hundred questions racing through her mind, she knew it was important to ask them in order. It would make all the difference when she spoke with the judge.

"What time did the call come in?"

Instead of answering, Christine walked over to the counter and retrieved the portable phone from its charger. "Eight fifty-one," she said, showing Sam the caller ID.

Sam jotted the number down in her notebook. She knew it would be easy to chase down the person who had made the call. The prison system did few things well, and recording calls was one of them. Flipping to a blank page, she asked where the diaries had been found.

"The person told me they were inside the air conditioning vent next to Megan's bed."

"And is that where you found them?" Sam asked, wishing the woman would just tell the story instead of starting and stopping every few seconds.

"Yes, they were pushed back into the pipe a ways."

"Did the caller tell you why your daughter wanted them removed?"

"She said that if I didn't destroy them, the police would find them and convict my daughter of murder. She said Megan would spend the rest of her life behind bars."

She got that part right, Sam thought. Once they retrieved the watch from Megan's home, the jury would have no other choice but to convict the woman.

Christine reached for the box of tissues. "I still can't believe she killed Aaron. I know she did, but I don't understand why. Even if he did cheat on her, that's no excuse to kill him."

"What makes you think your daughter killed him?" Sam asked.

The woman slid the second diary toward Sam. "She talks about him like she knows he's dead. It's all, 'he did this, or he did that,' nothing about what they might do if they see each other again. Look at this one," Christine said, pointing to one of the last entries.

For a second, Sam thought she was seeing things.

The final three pages were all about the baseball bat and how it was Aaron's fault it was gone. It wasn't hard to read between the lines.

"Do you know what happened to this bat Megan is talking about?" Sam asked.

"I have no idea. It used to hang on her wall, right above her bed. It's the one she used to hit the home run with during the state finals her senior year. She loved it more than life itself. She used to say that she was going to put it in one of those cases and keep it forever."

"When was the last time you remember seeing the bat?"

"I'm not a hundred percent sure. You have to remember that Megan was a teenager at the time. Back then, there were more bad days than there were good ones. We were always fighting about something, so it was rare that I would go into her bedroom. It may have gone missing before Aaron did or it could have been…" the woman didn't finish her statement.

Sam looked at the date the entry was made. If Megan was telling the truth, the bat had disappeared sometime before July sixth. Reading the passage again, Sam was convinced that Megan had gotten rid of the bat because she knew it would link her to the murder.

"Did your daughter have a favorite place where she liked to hang out back then?"

"I can't remember," Christine said, wiping the tears from her eyes. "I know for a while, she was into the street racing scene, but I have no idea where they used to do it. I just remember wishing she'd find a different hobby. One time, I even took her to the hospital with me, just to show her what could happen in a car accident, but it didn't have any effect on her."

"Have you read through all of these diaries?" Sam asked.

"I read the first one." Christine turned away from the books lying on the table. "I was hoping it would contain something to prove she was innocent, but…"

"I understand," Sam said, closing the diary. "I need to call my boss."

Chapter 52

"You're killing me," Jenna replied, when Sam told her about the new diaries. "We're not even sure if we're going to be able to use the first one, and now you're calling me about four new ones."

Sam could tell her boss wasn't happy. It wasn't like she blamed the woman. They were walking a tightrope made of thread. Instead of telling her what was contained in the diaries, she explained how the homeowner had come to find them.

"Have you traced the number yet?"

"I know it came from the jail, but we'll need a warrant for the call records to determine who made the call, but it proves Megan is trying to cover her tracks."

"I get it. Let me call the judge and see what he thinks."

After hanging up, Sam scrolled through her contact list until she found Carol's number. Like Jenna, the former prosecutor argued that they were deep into a grey area when it came to confiscating the diaries. Like it or not, ownership was still in question.

"You might be able to prove she's involved if you can find out who made the phone call. Once that person testifies that she was directed to place the phone call in question, you should be able to convince a judge that you need a search warrant for the diaries."

"You know as well as I do that getting phone records isn't easy," Sam said, feeling like they were once again fighting the system that was determined to protect the criminals at all costs. "Do you happen to know anyone who works at the women's prison?"

"I do," Carol replied.

Sam gave her the number and time the call was placed, then asked the former assistant district attorney to see if her friend could pull a few strings to find out who might have been using the phone at the time.

"You've been asking for a lot of favors these past couple of weeks. Are you sure this is the way you want to play it?"

Although she didn't like it, Sam knew why the woman was expressing concern. In their business, favors were more valuable than gold. When you were owed one, you could ask that person for anything in return. It didn't matter if it was outlandish or not.

"Maybe you're right," Sam said, not wanting to get herself in too deep. While it would take some time to get the phone records, they would get them. Prisoners gave up their right to privacy the moment they picked up the phone.

"I was thinking about our earlier conversation and realized we were looking at it the wrong way. We don't need to involve your neighbor. What if we used the Cotati Police instead?"

"What are you talking about?" Sam asked, trying to recall the conversation Carol was talking about.

"We were discussing a break in. If someone were to break into the daughter's home, the police would have to respond. The first thing they're going to do is determine if anything is missing. The only way to do that is to look through everything."

"I thought about that, but it still doesn't solve anything. If someone breaks into Megan's house, her lawyer is going to claim we had something to do with it because we couldn't get a warrant."

"Not if it were only one of a handful of houses that were broken into. Think about it. We could hit four or five of the houses in the neighborhood. We could even make it look like teenagers did it."

Sam started to object, then realized it could work. No one was living in Megan's home at the moment. Any thief canvassing the area would see it for what it was. An easy mark.

"Let's see what the judge says first."

"Fair enough," Carol replied. "Call me if anything changes." She paused for a few seconds, then told Sam that her name was being discussed in the San Francisco field office.

"How do you…" Sam stopped herself from asking the obvious question. Of course, Carol had ears inside the field office. "Should I be worried?"

"I wouldn't expect to get any Christmas cards from Special Agent White this year. Right now, they're just complaining about you ruining their investigation, but I don't expect them to do anything about it. By the way, have you heard from Agent Thurman yet?"

"Not a thing. Maybe she decided this case isn't worth taking."

"When I spoke with her last night, she said she'd be getting in touch with you first thing this morning. I'll call her again. See what the holdup is."

"Don't worry about it. If the judge decides we still don't have enough to get a warrant, we'll go with your idea to break into a few homes."

Sam dropped her phone into her pocket. Like it or not, it was time to deliver the bad news to Christine. As much as she wanted to confiscate the diaries and put an end to the case, she was going to have to wait for a judge to decide if they could be used in a court of law.

"Are you saying Megan could get away with this because I gave you the diary?" Christine asked, as she got out of the chair. "That's ridiculous. This is my house. I can give you anything I want."

"Yes and no." Sam indicated for Christine to sit down. "It's not as simple as who owns the house. The judge has to figure out whether or not Megan has the right to keep stuff here. She is your daughter after all."

"I threw her out of here when she turned eighteen."

"You've also let her stay here a number of times since then. She could argue that whatever she left behind still belongs to her, and you had no right to give it to anyone."

"That makes no sense. She's got a place of her own. Why would she need to keep this here unless she was planning on hiding it from the authorities?"

You've got a good point, Sam thought. She was about to tell Christine her opinion when her phone rang.

Chapter 53

"Bad news," Jenna said. "The judge is turning down our request for a search warrant. He says you should have waited for his decision before you went back to the house to talk to Megan's mother."

"You're kidding me. Why is this guy so determined to protect a murderer?" Sam paced back and forth beside her SUV as she considered her options. Part of her wanted to have the judge whacked.

"He claims there was a reasonable expectation of finding new evidence and you should have considered that before you went there. I'm sorry."

"I can't believe this guy is protecting her. She doesn't even live here."

"I feel the same way, but there's nothing we can do about it."

When the sergeant went quiet, Sam realized the other shoe was about to drop. Without the diaries, they had no evidence linking Megan to the crime. That meant the brass would force them to move the case to the cold files, which would all but guarantee the woman got away with murdering Aaron Burwell.

"As much as I hate to say it. It's time to move on," Jenna said.

"What about the feds? They might be able…"

"After what you did to their investigation, I doubt they're going to be willing to help us with anything anytime soon. I know this sucks, but we have other cases to work on. We've already dedicated too much time to this one."

"I understand," Sam said, thinking it was time to give Carol the go ahead to have someone break into Megan's home. "I'm going to let Christine know what's happening, then I'm going to take lunch. I'll see you soon."

The walk back to the front door was as painful as

any Sam had ever taken. Despite the proof, her department was giving up. All because some judge was too scared to do his job.

"You're not going to do anything?" Christine asked. "Why? You have the diaries."

"The judge won't let us use them. He says anything Megan left behind is privileged. Until we find something else linking her to the crime, there's nothing we can do."

"So because she hid the stuff here, you can't use it?"

"Pretty much," Sam replied, realizing how unfair it sounded. In a perfect world, the judge would have seen through Megan's plan.

"What if it wasn't here anymore? Could you use it then?"

"Under normal circumstances, yes. If someone throws something away, it becomes fair game. We no longer need their permission to look through it."

"Then I'll throw it away," Christine said, gathering up the diaries. "If you give me half an hour, I'll have everything she owns out of the house."

"It won't work." Sam reached out and grabbed Christine's arm. "The judge will claim we coerced you into getting rid of her stuff."

"So now I'm not even allowed to throw it away?"

"You could, but we won't be allowed to go through it." Sam got to her feet. Her intention was to get Christine to sit down. The woman was beginning to look a little lightheaded. "I know it's not fair, but it is what it is."

"Do you have a murderer keeping their stuff at your house?" The retired nurse waited for Sam to shake her head. "Then you have no idea what it's like for me. Either way, I want her stuff out of my house."

As the woman headed down the hallway toward her daughter's room, Sam called Jenna. She needed to give the sergeant a heads up.

"Did you ask her not to do it?"

"Of course," Sam replied. "I'm not a complete idiot."

"That's not what I meant. If she throws everything away, we'll never be able to prove that Megan murdered Aaron."

Sam could feel Jenna's frustration coming through the phone. It matched her own. They were about to lose the only thing they had linking Megan to the crime. Once it reached the landfill, that was it. The case was over.

"Ask her to give us twenty-four hours."

"Why?" Sam asked, knowing another day wouldn't make any difference. No judge in their right mind was going to side against Judge Bryan.

"Maybe I can get an injunction to keep her from throwing the stuff away."

"Did you bump your head on something?" Sam asked, keeping her voice low. "You can't punish her for this. She's not the one who messed up."

"She's tampering with evidence."

"Evidence they won't let us use. Forget it. I'm not going to let the system treat her like a criminal while they let the real criminal get away with murder."

The silence stretched until it became uncomfortable. Sam was about to hang up when she heard her boss let out a long sigh.

"You're right. We're not going to treat her like a criminal. Do me a favor. Once she gets everything outside, I want you to take a picture of it. I want to have it on hand when the public asks why we weren't able to catch Aaron's killer."

"That's brilliant," Sam said. "You just gave me an idea."

As if she could read Sam's mind, Jenna warned her to make sure that whatever she did couldn't come back to bite them in the butt.

"Don't worry. I'll be long gone before anything happens."

Chapter 54

The Last Call was packed when Sam arrived for lunch. Making her way to the seating area, Sam passed by several police officers who had their eyes glued to the televisions above the bar. They appeared to be transfixed on the headline scrolling along the bottom of the screens. The four major networks in the bay area along with both local news stations were all running the same story.

Sam paused to watch the news anchor, who was trying to explain to their viewers, why his crew was standing in front of a large pile of trash sitting in front of a home in Camden's second most exclusive neighborhood. In Sam's opinion, the story might have been compelling had it not been for the headline stating why they were there.

It had taken the media less than half an hour to find out it was Judge Bryan who refused to issue the search warrant. When the anchor mentioned his name, a picture of the judge appeared in the upper righthand corner of the screen. It showed him sitting in the area's most famous French restaurant, dining with a bunch of politicians, including the lieutenant governor.

Smooth, Sam thought.

Nothing upset the voters more, than showing politicians gathered together, eating three-hundred-dollar dinners while the rest of the world struggled to make their mortgage payment. Sam figured it wouldn't take long for the judge to buckle under the weight of the bad publicity.

"Can you believe it?" the waitress asked, as she sat a glass of water in front of Sam. "They're saying that judge is protecting a murderer."

"It happens more often than you think," Sam replied. "Can I get a barbecue bacon burger and a Pepsi?"

"Sure thing," the woman said, jotting her order down. "If you ask me, it isn't right for him to protect that woman. Everyone knows she killed that guy."

Sam nodded as she reached for her phone.

"Holy crap, Sam. When I said take a picture, I didn't mean for you to send it to the media."

"I didn't send it to anyone but you," Sam replied. Her attention was still on the television screens. "Have you heard from Judge Bryan yet?"

"The phones have been ringing off the hook for the last half hour. Everyone wants us to confirm the story. Who gave them Megan's name?" Jenna asked.

"I'm guessing Christine did. I left the house right after I sent you the picture of her stuff." Sam didn't mention that she had helped the retired nurse carry it out of the house. "What'd the lieutenant say?"

"He and the chief are still on the phone with the governor's office. I asked you to make sure this didn't blow up in our face."

"I'm watching the news right now. No one's mentioned our names yet."

"Yet being the key word. It's not going to take them long to find out who's in charge of this case. I expect you to say, 'no comment' when they ask you about the story."

"You got it boss."

Although Jenna didn't say it, Sam could tell her boss was happy with the media coverage. So far, the department was looking like the good guys. As long as the wind didn't shift, they had nothing to worry about. Laying the phone on the table, Sam turned her attention back to the news.

One of the local reporters was asking Christine why she felt it necessary to throw all of her daughter's belongings away. It was a slight variation on the other questions asked, but it brought the topic back around to Judge Bryan.

The moment Christine stopped speaking, the shot of the judge eating dinner with the politicians reappeared on the screen. Below it, the headline said, "County Judge dines out while killer remains loose." A blatant disregard for the truth, but that was the point. They wanted to ensure the public got riled up.

"Why haven't the police arrested your daughter?" the reporter asked. "If what you're saying is true, she's a murderer."

"I tried to give them everything I had," Christine

said, "but the detective couldn't take it. The judge told her it wasn't admissible or something. All because I'm her mother."

Just as an image of Megan appeared on the screen, Sam's phone began to ring. Thinking it was a reporter wanting to confirm the story, she answered.

"Is this Detective Wright?"

"It is," Sam replied. "How can I help you?"

"I'm Special Agent Lisa Thurman. I'm calling you about a cold case I hear you're working on. Is this a good time to talk?"

"Sorry to waste your time, but it doesn't look like we're going to need your help after all," Sam said, before explaining that the story was being plastered all over the news.

"If it's all the same, I wouldn't mind talking to you about it."

Sam assumed it was because the woman wanted to take the credit once Megan was arrested. Any other time, she'd have told the federal agent to pound sand, but with all the media coverage, she figured it would make things better if the feds were involved.

"Sure, why not? When can you get here?"

"I just left San Francisco," Lisa replied. "According to my GPS, I should be there in about an hour and a half. How about I meet you at the station?"

"That'll work. See you then."

Chapter 55

The federal agent was sitting in the briefing room with Amy when Sam arrived. The two were talking and laughing with each other like they were old friends.

"You really jumped off a bridge to arrest someone?" Amy asked, shaking her head in amazement.

"It worked, too. The suspects were so focused on me, they never saw the other agents approaching their boat. By the time my team pulled me from the river, the bad guys were already in cuffs."

They both turned as Sam came into the room.

"Hi," Lisa said, as she got to her feet. "I'm Special Agent Thurman. You must be Detective Wright. It's a pleasure to meet you."

Sam glanced at her watch, wondering how the federal agent beat her to the station. Even without traffic, it should have taken the woman closer to two hours to get from San Francisco to Camden. As if she were able to read her mind, Lisa claimed she had fractured the speed limit once or twice along the way.

Ignoring the agent's statement, Sam asked her if she had gotten the chance to look at the file yet. Just because the woman appeared to be nice, she didn't want her hanging around any longer than necessary.

"Sgt. Richards thought it would be best if we waited for you," Lisa said, taking her seat.

Before Sam had a chance to point out that she was right on time, Jenna came into the room carrying hard copies of all their reports. After passing them out, she turned on the computer and pulled up the images taken from the first diary.

The agent didn't bother looking up at the screen. Her attention was focused on the file in her hands. When she managed to pull herself away from it, she asked Sam why she felt Megan was responsible for Aaron's death.

"She's the only one who had motive and opportunity." Sam looked back and forth between Amy and Jenna to see if they were going to back her up. "After we eliminated the other suspects, we took a long look at Megan. That's when her mother remembered she used to keep a diary."

"It's unusual for a teenage girl to kill her boyfriend. What reason did she have to kill him?"

"According to her diary, she believed he was cheating on her. Her original plan was to lure him to the property, then call the cops on him."

"Because of the drugs?" Lisa asked. Her eyes were scanning the report again. "Is there any chance the person who was growing the marijuana caught Mr. Burwell on his property and killed him?"

"Not according to her diary," Sam said, feeling like the federal agent was questioning her investigative skills. "The day after Aaron went missing, Megan began referring to him in the past tense. She also mentions losing her favorite bat because of him."

"Where is that?"

"In the diaries we weren't able to obtain." Sam slid

her body camera over to Jenna. "I took as many pictures as I could."

While not the best quality images, they were good enough to reveal the handwriting on the pages. Amy was the first to note how eerie it was to read the circumstances surrounding the disappearance.

"Sounds like a confession to me," the detective said, reading one of the sentences aloud. "She all but confesses to killing him."

"Why didn't she confess?" Lisa asked. "If she never expected anyone to read these journals, why not just come out and say she killed him?"

No one had an answer. Sam had to admit that it was a bit odd to not confess to the crime after spending all the time talking about how you'd pull it off. Then she remembered the most famous murder case in the last fifty years.

"Maybe this was going to be her 'How I'd do it' book. Like the one O.J. wrote after his acquittal."

"That's a possibility. These are pretty detailed plans. She even talks about what she's going to do after she has him arrested." The agent asked Jenna to flip to the next image. "Does she ever come right out and say that he's dead?"

"No," Sam said. "But look at the way she talks about him. All of it's in the past tense. I've talked to plenty of people who have lost a loved one. They all refer to them as if they're still alive. It takes them time to accept they're gone."

"Show me the one that mentions the murder weapon."

As the agent read the entry, Sam kept glancing at her phone. The news of Judge Bryan refusing to grant a search warrant was all over social media. It seemed like everyone had an opinion on the subject. Most didn't understand why the judge would rule in Megan's favor, while others supported his decision, claiming the justice system had gotten one right.

"Does the mother remember seeing the bat after Aaron went missing?" Lisa asked. "I want to make sure it wasn't found a month later in the garage or something."

"She doesn't remember ever seeing the bat again but can't swear as to when it went missing. All we have for a timeline is Megan's diaries."

Lisa pointed at the screen. "It doesn't say when it went missing, just that it was. For all we know, Aaron could have taken it weeks prior to his disappearance."

"Then why wait until the sixth to write about it. According to her mother, Megan was planning to keep this bat forever. She used it in the state finals or something."

"If it was special, why use it to kill her boyfriend? Why not use a tire iron or a golf club?"

"Maybe because her plan wasn't to kill him. We're thinking she wanted to stick to her original plan and have him arrested. But for one reason or another, they get into an argument, and she whacks him with the baseball bat."

"Why take the bat if she wasn't planning on killing him?"

"The same reason why people carry a gun. Maybe she planned on confronting him about the affair and felt that it was wise to have the bat on hand in case he got angry."

"Do we know how they got from the lake to the place where his body was found?" Lisa asked. "I'm assuming they didn't walk."

"She had a two-hour window to kill him and get

back to the lake before she reported him missing. We're assuming they drove out there together, then she drove back alone."

"It's all circumstantial, but I can see why you'd want a search warrant for both properties. If she left the diaries behind, there's a chance she left something else." Lisa pulled her phone out and dialed someone's number. "Let me see if I can't pull a string or two and get this case back on track."

Chapter 56

Four hours later, Sam was standing outside of Megan's home watching the members of the Cotati Police Department clear the place. Although the small agency didn't have dedicated detectives, she knew they were well trained in forensics and more than capable of searching the home.

While they waited for the initial search to be completed, Sam kept thinking about how Lisa had worked the system to get the warrant. Unlike the other feds she had worked with, Special Agent Thurman was all business. She was a single focus kind of woman. It was a sight to behold.

When the first officer came out of the home, he gave

them the "all clear" sign, indicating it was safe to enter and begin a more thorough search of the property.

Dividing the home into four sections, Sam and Amy volunteered to take the kitchen. They were still going through the cabinets when she heard one of the officers shout that they had found something. It was hard not to rush into the bedroom to find out what it was.

A few seconds later, the officer came out and asked them to join him. When they walked into the room, he pointed at a hole in the floor. Peering into the empty space, Sam saw a metal baseball bat. She couldn't believe her eyes. While it was too much to hope that it was the murder weapon, she couldn't stop herself from wanting it to be.

"There might be some blood on the grip, but I can't be sure until we test it."

"If you don't mind, I'd like our analyst to run the test," Sam said, motioning for Amy to call Bobbi inside. "The fewer people who touch it, the better."

"No worries, detective." He took a step to his right and snapped another picture of the hole in the floor. "Think it could be the murder weapon?"

Leaning as close to the bat as possible, Sam nodded. While she couldn't imagine why Megan would have kept the item, she couldn't deny it matched the description of the bat the teenager had used in high school.

"You rang," Bobbi said, entering the room.

Sam backed away from the hole in the floor. "We may have found the murder weapon."

The crime scene analyst photographed the bat from every angle before lifting it from its hiding spot. Laying it on the floor, she took more photos, before reaching into her kit and pulling out some swabs.

"Looks like there might be some blood in the weave," she said, using the end of the swab to point it out. "Hold on." She sat the swab down and pulled a small flashlight from her pocket. "I've got a hair."

Although it wasn't necessary, everyone held their breath as the crime scene analyst removed the hair. An audible sigh was heard as it was dropped into an evidence bag.

"What'd you find?" Lisa asked, as she poked her head inside the room.

"A baseball bat," Sam answered. "Bobbi also recovered a hair and is about to test the bat for blood."

The federal agent waved Sam over to the door. "Your report mentioned something about a possible watch or bracelet. I think we found it."

Following her across the hall, Sam felt a wave of relief wash over her when she saw the watch sitting on top of an evidence bag.

"Where'd you find it?"

"In that vent," Lisa replied, pointing to the ceiling. "There's an inscription on the back. We're going to need Aaron's mother to confirm it's the same watch."

Sam nodded as she bent over to look at the gold watch. It took everything she had to keep from smiling. Her plan had worked. It wouldn't matter if the bat was the murder weapon or not. With the watch, they'd have everything needed to ensure that Megan spent the rest of her life behind bars.

"There's something else," Lisa said, motioning for Sam to follow her. "Look under the bed."

Getting down onto her knees, Sam peered into the darkness. At first she didn't see anything. Then a sliver of something white caught her eye.

"What is it?"

"I think it's a photograph, but it's stuck to the frame." Lisa moved to the head of the bed. "Help me lift the mattress.

On the count of three, they lifted the old mattress off the frame, then carried it to the other side of the room, where they leaned it against the closet.

Sam was on pins and needles as they made their way back to the bed frame. Letting the agent take the lead, Sam did her best to stay out of the woman's way as she photographed the picture.

"How long do you think it's been there?" Sam asked.

"Years," Lisa replied. She tugged on the corner of the photograph again. "It's not coming off. Aaron went missing on the fourth of July, right?"

"Yeah. He was reported missing around eleven o'clock."

"Is this him?"

Although the picture was bent and faded, it wasn't hard for Sam to recognize the individuals smiling at the camera. It was Aaron and Megan. The photographer had managed to snap the picture at just the right moment to capture the fireworks in the background.

"This must have been taken an hour or two before he was killed." Sam pointed to the burst of light over Megan's shoulder. "We know the fireworks started at nine."

"Congrats, Detective. It looks like you solved the case."

Chapter 57

Shades of pink were showing in the east when Sam pulled away from the home. As tired as she was, there was still work to do. First on her list was speaking with Aaron's mother. The woman had been waiting more than two decades for answers. While some of the evidence collected would take weeks to process, Sam felt confident that she had enough to deliver the good news to the grieving mother.

As she drove west, Sam wondered about the bat. According to the diary, it had gone missing around the time of Aaron's disappearance.

"Why keep it?" Sam asked herself.

No matter how she tried to justify it in her mind,

none of the answers made any sense. Keeping the bat was beyond stupid. Now all they had to do was match the blood and hair sample to the victim. Sam was still thinking about the bat when her phone started ringing.

"Tell me the good news," Jenna said.

"Didn't Amy call you?" Sam asked, putting the phone on speaker.

"She did, but I want to hear your take on it. I heard you may have found the murder weapon."

"It looks like it, but I'm not getting my hopes up." Sam fell silent as she passed a slow-moving truck. "I can't figure out why she'd keep the bat."

"You said it was special to her. Didn't she win some big game with it?"

"Yeah, but still. Would you keep the murder weapon?"

"I wouldn't, but I know how forensics works. No matter how well you clean something, there's always something left behind. A drop of blood here, a bead of sweat there. It's always something that links the weapon to the crime."

"That's my point," Sam said. "Megan may not be

the sharpest knife in the drawer, but she's not stupid. She's had almost twenty-five years to get rid of it." Then she remembered thinking the same thing when the mayor revealed that he had kept the watch.

"Some people just don't know how to let go of things." The sergeant went on to explain how she had a few family members who seemed to collect the weirdest things, including tv guides. It wasn't done because they thought the items would be worth something one day. For each person, the joy of hoarding the items was what gave them pleasure.

"I guess," Sam said, slowing down as she approached the Burwell home. "I gotta go. I'll call you after I talk to Aaron's mother."

"You should start by telling her that we found the killer."

Sam hung up without replying. In her heart, she knew it wouldn't make any difference to Mrs. Burwell. Knowing who the killer was, wasn't going to bring her son back to life. If anything, it would only cause the woman more grief to find out that her son's murderer was someone who claimed to have loved him.

Parking next to an old Buick, Sam considered how best to share the good news. The last thing she wanted to do was make it sound as if all the woman's troubles were over. Although they had recovered his body, some of his personal items, and discovered the identity of the killer, there was still a long way to go before the dust settled.

Murder trials were never easy. To start with, they took time. If Megan wanted to, she could drag the case out for years. Not that it would matter in the end. There was more than enough evidence to convict her. The delay would come because the system was designed to take time. It afforded people with every opportunity to prove their innocence, even when there was none.

The sound of a screen door closing took Sam from her thoughts. Reaching for the door handle, she slid out of her SUV and started toward the woman standing on the front porch.

"If you're here to search my house again, you're going to have to wait until I get back from work. My boss says he'll fire me if I miss another day."

"No ma'am, I'm not here to search your house." Sam fought to get the words out. "I came to tell you that we know who killed your son."

"Was it Megan?"

Sam nodded. The joy she had expected was nowhere to be found. Somehow, getting justice for Aaron wasn't enough for her. She wanted the woman to pay with her life.

"Are you sure it was her?" Mrs. Burwell asked.

"We are," Sam replied, as she handed the grieving mother her tablet. "I need to know if you've ever seen this watch before."

"It's the one I gave my husband after we were married." The tears ran down her cheeks as she studied the image. He loved that watch. So did Aaron."

Reaching over, Sam tapped the right-hand side of the screen, bringing up the next photo. It was a close up shot of the engraving.

"Do you recognize this image?"

Mrs. Burwell handed the tablet back to Sam before heading back into the home.

"I'm sorry," Sam said, as the door was closed in her face. Not that she blamed the woman for going inside. If their situations were reversed, Sam felt as if she would have done the same thing. There was no point in discussing the matter further.

Turning around, Sam headed back to her Explorer. She'd have to wait until the trial was over, but swore that once it was, Megan would get what was coming to her.

Chapter 58

Sam got a hero's welcome when she returned to the station. Even the chief managed to come downstairs and shake her hand as she crossed the bullpen. It made her wonder if it was because she had proved that Megan was the killer or if he was doing it to show everyone that he never had any doubt.

"We're all proud of you, Detective," he said, squeezing her hand. "We knew you would close this case."

It took everything Sam had to keep from rolling her eyes at the man. With a quick nod to acknowledge his praise, she thanked him for his faith in her, then turned toward the detective's wing. If all had gone well during her absence, they should have an arrest warrant for Megan Johnson, and she wanted to be the one who picked the woman up.

When she reached the briefing room, she saw her boss sitting at the table with Lisa. The two looked as if they had swallowed a bug.

"What's going on?" she asked, as she entered the room. "Please don't tell me we have a problem."

"No problem," Lisa said. "Just making the arrangements for our lab to conduct the analysis on what we found at Mrs. Johnson's home."

"What's wrong with letting Bobbi handle it?" Sam asked, thinking the federal agent wanted her people to do the analysis in order to hog all the glory.

"Ms. Harris asked for our assistance." Lisa slid another sheet of paper toward Jenna before turning her attention back to Sam. "I'm not trying to step on anyone's toes here."

"No, you just want to take all the credit."

The special agent shook her head. "As far as I'm concerned, you're the one who deserves all the credit. You're the one who identified the suspect. All I'm trying to do is help you close it out. But if you'd rather wait weeks or months to get the labs back, by all means, be my guest."

Sam studied the woman's face for any sign of deception. If she was lying, Sam couldn't tell.

"I'm sorry. I shouldn't have questioned your motives."

"Don't worry about it," Lisa said, waving away the apology. "We're all tired. How did it go with the mother?"

"Like you'd expect. She identified the watch, then asked me several times if we were sure Megan did it. I think she's having a hard time coming to grips with her son's girlfriend being the murderer."

Lisa motioned for Sam to take a seat. "What about you? Do you think we have the right person?"

"No doubt about it," Sam said, glancing over at Jenna. Something in the sergeant's demeanor was giving her cause for concern. "What's going on?"

"Megan's lawyer is on the warpath. She's claiming the search was illegal because we leaked the story to the press in order to get the warrant." Jenna paused to write her initials on the form sitting in front of her. "She's also claiming someone planted the evidence."

"Which one of us is she blaming?" Sam asked, knowing there wasn't a judge in the county who would listen to the woman.

"You," Jenna said. "Claims you've had it out for her ever since her husband popped you in the mouth." The sergeant held up her hand to keep Sam from replying. "We know it's not possible, but I think it might be best if you let Amy take the lead from here on out."

"That's fine with me." Sam stopped long enough to look at the white boards. "Have we gotten the arrest warrant yet?"

"Yep. James and Marsha are on their way up to the prison as we speak. She'll be brought back here for questioning, then she'll face the judge in the morning."

Sam turned to Lisa. "How long is it going to take your guys to run the blood and DNA tests?"

"We should have it back within a week."

Wow, Sam thought. In her experience, anything less than a month was cause for celebration. Then another thought hit her. If Megan wasn't willing to plead guilty, she could have her family lean on her. No one ever refused an order from them. At least not twice.

"Why don't you go ahead and call it a day," Jenna said. "There's nothing left here for you to do."

"Sounds good," Sam replied, heading for the door. She was about to open it when she realized that Lisa had never expressed her opinion on the case. Turning around, she asked the agent if she believed they had arrested the right person.

"Based on what we have, I'd say she's guilty. We'll know more once the lab is finished. By the way, I'm also sending the diaries and the locket you found."

"I forgot all about those." Sam glanced over at Jenna who was still focused on the growing pile of paperwork sitting in front of her. "Has anyone gone through the stuff Christine threw out?"

"I have Bobbi working on it."

"That's why you're the boss," Sam said, walking out of the room.

Instead of leaving through the front or side doors, Sam went out the back. While it would take her longer to reach her vehicle, it put her closer to the lab. She had some questions for the crime scene analyst, beginning with why she'd let the feds take over the processing of the evidence.

Although Sam had to admit the feds were faster at getting results, they were also glory hounds. It didn't matter which agency it was they'd all do whatever it took to get their names in the press. She suspected it was because they felt the need to justify their existence.

More often than not, the cops at the top of the food chain relied on the state and city agencies to close their cases for them. In many ways, they were no different than vultures. Scavengers, picking up after the hard work was finished.

Pulling the lab door open, Sam announced her arrival before stepping inside. It was a habit she had picked up after spooking one of the techs. While everyone had walked away unscathed, the incident with the scalpel still gave her nightmares.

Chapter 59

"If you're here looking for results, you're too late. I've already packed up everything," Bobbi said, handing a box to one of her assistants. "We're shipping everything to Quantico."

"I heard." Sam sat down at the analyst's desk. "What made you decide to let them handle it?"

"Maybe you haven't heard, but we were backed up long before Aaron's skeleton was found in Sgt. Edwards old house."

Sam nodded. No one had to tell her how much work they all had. It seemed like every day they fell a little further behind. Looking around at the men and women in the lab, it was a wonder anyone went to jail. It only happened because no one wanted a speedy trial.

"Can you at least tell me if the bat had blood on it or not?"

"It did." Bobbi handed her a sheet of paper. "I was able to match the blood type, but that was it. You'll have to wait for the feds if you want anything more than that."

"Can you tell me anything about the hair you found on it?" Sam asked, realizing that she was putting too much pressure on the analyst.

"All I can say is that it belonged to a human. Before you ask, it was consistent with the hair we obtained with the skeleton."

"One last question. How long do you think the bat was in the house?"

The analyst stopped what she was doing and turned to face Sam. "What are you trying to ask me?"

"Is there any chance it was planted in the last few days?"

"If it was, whoever planted it knew what they were doing." Bobbi walked over and tapped on her keyboard, bringing up a picture of the bat. "See this?"

Sam looked at the close-up picture of the dirt which

had settled on the end of the bat. While it didn't mean anything to her, she assumed it meant something to the crime scene analyst.

"This dirt came from the floor." Bobbi could see that the detective wasn't following her. "Over time, dirt and dust settles between the pieces of wood which makes up the floor. As you walk over it, it rains down on anything beneath it."

"So you're saying this bat had been sitting under the floor for years."

"At least a dozen," Bobbi replied. "The odds of someone knowing how to fake that, are slim and none."

"What about the watch?"

"That was different. It looks like it was pulled out on a regular basis. We didn't find any fingerprints on it, but we did find what looks like skin cells on the knob you'd use to wind it."

I wonder how they managed that? Sam asked herself. She had to give it to her cousin's men. When they set out to frame someone, they thought of everything.

"I guess I'll let you get back to it then," Sam said, getting out of the chair.

"You wouldn't happen to be heading to that fancy Italian place for lunch, would you?"

"The only place I'm going, is home." Sam was almost to the door when she realized why the analyst was asking. "I'll call and have them send something over."

Without thinking, Sam dialed Luca's office number instead of the main line. The old Italian answered on the first ring.

"It's about time you called to check up on me," he said. "I was beginning to think that you had forgotten about me."

"Never," Sam said, sliding behind the wheel of her Explorer. "When did you get back?"

"Yesterday."

Sam could detect a note of sadness in his voice. When she asked how things were going, the chef informed her that his mother had indeed succumbed to the cancer. In spite of everything, he was glad that he had gotten the chance to see her before she passed.

"Is there anything you need?" she asked, thinking her father would have already sent his men over to take care of anything the old Italian needed.

"I'm good. This was not unexpected. How are things with you? I heard you were working some old murder case."

"It's done now." Sam paused to look both ways before pulling out onto the street. "If it's not too much trouble, can you send a half dozen lunch specials over to our lab?"

"Anything else?"

"Better throw in four more for the detective's," she added. "I'll stop by later to tip the staff."

"How many times do I need to tell you that your money's no good here? If you keep spoiling them, they'll come to expect it."

Sam knew better than to argue with the man. In his mind, the Carlucci's should never have to pay for anything. It stemmed from his time in the old country. According to Luca, he would have never survived if it had not been for Sam's grandfather.

"I gotta go," she said. "I'll come by tomorrow night for dinner."

"Should I set a place for two?"

For a second, Sam thought about asking him to reserve a single spot for her, then she realized it would only lead to more questions, so she told him to keep to his standard routine. She figured she could always invite Amy to join her.

Sliding her thumb across the end button, Sam made a mental note to talk to her father about Luca. It was clear that the old man was suffering from the loss of his mother and needed some kind of pick me up. She thought about a party but knew he wouldn't want that. Dinners were also out of the question. No one would want to cook for the chef, lest their food be judged.

"What am I doing?" Sam asked herself when she remembered that she had already spoken to her father about it.

Pulling to the side of the road, Sam put the Explorer into park and got out of the vehicle. The weariness she was feeling in her mind, had crept into her bones. Unsure of what to do, she called Carol and asked her to send one of her men over to drive her home.

"Are you okay?" the bar owner asked.

"I'm just tired." Sam leaned up against the passenger side door of her SUV. She knew that if she shut her eyes for more than a second, she'd fall asleep. "I shouldn't be behind the wheel."

"I'll come get you myself. You can sleep in my office."

Sam started to tell the woman it wasn't necessary when she heard gravel crunching. Pulling the phone away from her ear, she stepped in front of her vehicle just in case it was someone who might be holding a grudge against the police. Her heart skipped a beat when she saw who it was.

"I'll call you right back," Sam said, as Special Agent in Charge Gary White approached.

"Car trouble?" he asked, glancing inside the SUV.

The anger at seeing him gave her the energy she needed to stay awake. "What are you doing here, Agent White?"

Gary held up both hands. "I was on my way to apologize, when I saw you sitting on the side of the road." With his eyes locked on her, he moved to the front of the vehicle. "Listen, I was wrong to be upset with you. It wasn't your fault that you didn't know about our operation. I should have given you guys a heads up."

"Yes, you should have. I wasted days trying to figure out who was starting the game back up. All because you weren't able to pick up the phone."

"Let me make it up to you. Have you eaten yet?"

Every fiber of her being wanted to tell the man to leave her alone, yet she couldn't bring herself to do it. Something about the federal agent got her blood flowing. Thinking she had just enough energy to make it to the Last Call, she suggested they go there for lunch.

"I was thinking we could go to L'ultima cena, but the Last Call will do," he said, walking over to open her door. "Lead the way."

Chapter 60

The moment they stepped into the bar; Sam realized her mistake. Everything they said to each other would be recorded and analyzed by her father's men. For a second, she thought about suggesting they go somewhere else, but deep down, she knew she'd never make it. Her body needed rest.

"Two barbecue bacon burgers and two Pepsi's," Gary said to the waitress, as they made their way over to an empty booth. "So how's your murder case going?"

"James is on his way to arrest the subject," Sam said, resisting the desire to close her eyes. "Turns out, it was the victim's girlfriend."

"I heard the press conference her mother made yesterday. Whoever set that up is a genius. The jury is going to know she's guilty before the D.A. finishes giving their opening statement."

"It helps that we recovered the murder weapon." Sam felt her eyes beginning to sag. "Do you know Special Agent Lisa Thurman?"

"I know of her." Gary leaned forward and took Sam's hands into his own. "Can you forgive me for threatening you? If it helps, I didn't mean it. I'd never have you arrested."

Yeah right, Sam thought. *If you knew who I was, you'd call every federal agent west of the Mississippi to come arrest me.*

"I mean it," he said, letting go of her hands.

Ignoring his statement, Sam asked him what he knew about the other federal agent. She could sense the woman was more than she seemed.

"If you believe the talk around the watercooler, she's the best profiler who ever lived. Last I heard, she's been focusing on cold cases."

"Is she a glory hound?"

"Not that I know of. Are you afraid she's going to take the credit for closing your case?" Gary held up a finger to indicate the waitress was heading in their direction. After thanking the young woman, he asked Sam why she was so interested in Lisa.

"She's not like the other feds I've met," Sam said, knowing Gary would take it to heart. "The woman seems to have a sixth sense or something."

"I don't know about that, but she does clear a lot of cases." He stopped speaking long enough to eat one of his fries. "How do you think she does it?"

"She didn't do much in this case, but I get the feeling she could have solved it whether we helped or not. Like I said, she seems to know things. It's weird."

"People say the same thing about you. I have to tell you; you've made quite the name for yourself over the last few years. I'm a little surprised you're still with a small agency."

Sam didn't know what to say. It wasn't like she could tell him the truth. If anyone figured out why she had been so successful, she'd be thrown in prison so fast, her head would spin.

"Has anyone tried to poach you yet?" he asked.

"I've gotten an offer or two," Sam replied, wishing she had a way to change the subject. "Camden may be small, but they keep me busy."

Gary took a bite of his burger, then explained why he was curious about her status. Like others in the law enforcement community, his bosses had taken notice of her success rate and were interested in talking to her about her future.

"No way," Sam said, pushing her plate to the edge of the table. "I have no desire whatsoever to become a fed. Get that idea out of your head right now."

"Is there a reason why?"

Where do I start?

As much as Sam wanted to list the reasons, she knew if she started down that particular road, she'd end up saying something which would get her in trouble, so she kept her mouth shut.

Gary wasn't ready to give up. He kept pressing her until she explained that she liked being a big fish in a tiny pond. In her opinion, staying with a small agency made the most sense.

"If I went to work for another agency, they'd make me start all over. I don't know about you, but I have no desire to go back to working the street as a patrol cop."

"Lateral transfers happen all the time." Gary plucked a fry from her plate. "Have you thought about seeing what's available in the city?"

The thought of working in San Francisco frightened Sam. Not because she thought it was too hard or too dangerous. She was afraid because the city belonged to her father. If she took a job with the SFPD, it would only be a matter of time before she was charged with investigating the man.

"I don't think so," she said. "They don't like to put people in jail down there."

"Don't believe everything you see on the news. If San Francisco isn't to your liking, how about the LAPD? I'm sure they'd love to have someone with your track record on their team."

"What are you, my recruiter? Why are you trying to convince me to leave Camden?" The first thing that popped in Sam's mind was his desire to restart the illegal poker game.

"You're wasting your talent in this one-horse town. If you don't get out now, you may not get the chance. Is this where you want to spend the rest of your life?"

Sam sat back and ran a hand over her face. Her head felt as if it were filled with cotton. She knew if she didn't put an end to the conversation soon, she'd end up promising to do something she had no desire to do. Although she had no desire to work for the SFPD, there were other big agencies she wouldn't mind checking out.

"I'm happy where I'm at, thank you very much." Sam pulled two twenties from her purse and dropped them on the table. "Now if you'll excuse me, I need to visit the little girl's room. Then I'm going home. It was nice seeing you again."

"Think about what I said." Gary got up and put his jacket on. "There's a great big world out there. Don't let it pass you by."

Chapter 61

"What are you smiling about?" Sam asked, as she entered Carol's office.

"You like him," she replied.

Sam wanted to deny it, but the words wouldn't come out of her mouth. For reasons she couldn't quite explain, the federal agent intrigued her. He was unlike anyone she had ever met. Although there was no chance of them becoming a couple, she did like to fantasize about it. In her mind, she could picture them living in a small well-appointed home overlooking the Pacific Ocean.

"Is it still okay if I crash here for a little while?"

"Sure," Carol said, handing her a key card. "I'll have one of my guys move your car to the public lot around the corner."

"Just make sure no one sees them driving it." Sam started toward the door when another thought hit her. "Would you be disappointed with me if I took a job with one of the larger agencies?"

"I thought you were going to go to work for the family?"

"I am." Sam paused to think about her question. The decision had been made. She was going to give up her current life, then take her rightful place by her father's side. "Never mind, I'm just tired."

"For what it's worth, I wouldn't be disappointed with you. A bit sad perhaps, but not disappointed. Just because I'd give my right arm to lead this family, doesn't mean it's the right thing for you. If you want to stick with being a cop, that's okay."

Despite being dead on her feet, Sam walked back over and dropped into one of the chairs in front of Carol's desk. The confusion about what to do with her life was driving her nuts. Deep down, she loved being a cop. She was making a difference. She wasn't sure she could get that same satisfaction by being a mobster.

"Do you think my dad will be disappointed?"

"Never. Your father loves you more than anything. He just wants you to be happy. Trust me, he'll support you no matter what you do."

Sam wasn't so sure. Even though he was the reason she was a cop, she could tell that he wanted her to give it up and take over the family.

"The only reason Gary is pushing you to take a chance with another agency is because he doesn't know all the facts."

"What do you mean?" Sam sensed there was a hidden message in the former prosecutor's statement. It almost sounded as if she knew the man.

"Look at this from his point of view. He knows your talents are being wasted here in Camden. The department is too small. The crimes, too pedestrian."

"I just closed a twenty-four-year-old cold case. How is that pedestrian?"

"Since you joined the department, you've worked two murder cases. In a bigger city, you could do that every week."

"That's true," Sam said, rubbing her eyes.

Camden was never going to experience the types of crimes which happened in the major metropolitan areas. While they dealt with major crimes on a regular basis, her biggest cases involved missing children. Most of which were runaways.

"Gary's a cop and he thinks like one. From his perspective, everyone should want to work for one of the big-name agencies. NYPD. LAPD. Chicago PD. To him, Camden is no different than Mayberry."

"He asked me if I wanted to be a fed."

"I heard." Carol tilted her head toward the bank of video monitors which took up the entire main wall of her office. "He wouldn't have suggested that, if he knew you had a chance to take over the family."

"How would he know?" Even as the question left her mouth, Sam realized there was only one way he could have known. *He works for my father.*

"That's my point," Carol said. "He doesn't know you have other opportunities, so he's thinking you should take a job with one of the big outfits like the SFPD."

Sam was confused. One minute, Carol was making

it sound like Gary knew she was part of the family. The next, she was acting like he had no clue.

Could I have been wrong?

Replaying the conversation in her head, she wasn't sure. Nothing was making sense. Getting to her feet, Sam thanked Carol for all her help, then proceeded toward the exit. The problem with Gary would have to wait for another day.

When she stepped into the hallway, Sam looked both ways before turning right. The small office Carol used as a spare bedroom was located in the back of the building. It had all the creature comforts of home, including a mini bar containing some choice bottles of scotch.

"He's not a gangster," Sam told herself, as she entered the small room.

The voice in the back of her mind disagreed. Before she could stop to think, she recalled how he had acted when they were in Vegas. At every turn, he had protected her. Only someone familiar with who she was, would have done that.

"It's not possible." Sam knew she was lying to herself. Her father had flipped many people since becoming the godfather of the Bongino family. Blackmail was his specialty. A number of times he had claimed there was no one he couldn't manipulate.

In her heart, Sam knew that everyone had their price. Gary was no different. While he might not sell his soul for cash, he might give it away in order to protect someone.

"Is that why you did it?"

The darkness didn't provide her with an answer.

Pushing the thoughts from her mind, Sam laid down on the bed and prayed that she was wrong.

Chapter 62

"What time is it?" Sam asked, staring up at Carol.

"A little after seven. I figured that you'd want to be out of here before the dinner rush begins." She handed Sam her keys. "If you slip out the back, no one will see you."

Sam reached over and picked up her phone. She had two missed text messages. The first was from Jenna letting her know Megan had been arrested for murder and the other was from Lisa asking if she had time to meet.

I wonder what she wants.

As far as Sam knew, the case was closed. While it would be nice to get a confession, it wasn't needed. They had more than enough evidence to convict Megan. No jury was going to let her walk. Not after her own mother had accused her of committing the crime.

Putting her shoes on, Sam thanked Carol again, then asked if she had spoken with Luca since he got back.

"I got a call from him last night letting me know he was back in town. I could tell he wasn't happy about being back."

"What do you mean?"

"Luca has always been close to his family. If it were up to him, we'd have moved them all here decades ago, but they won't leave Italy. Now that his mom is gone, he's afraid what little connection he has with them will disappear."

"Then why doesn't he move back there?" Sam asked, realizing it was a stupid question.

Luca had been on the run when he met her grandfather. For reasons which had never been explained, the chef had managed to upset one of the biggest crime families in Italy. It was only through sheer luck that he had escaped their wrath.

"There are still some people who remember what he did," Carol said. "It's the main reason why he doesn't visit more often. In spite of his connection with your father, there are still some people who may decide it's worth taking him out if they were given the opportunity."

Sam was shocked. No one went against Tony Carlucci. The man would have you killed for just thinking about it.

"You better go," Carol said, waiting for Sam to follow her.

Taking one last look to make sure she had everything, Sam wondered what kind of crime Luca could have committed to get himself put on a death list. He didn't seem like the kind of guy who would upset people on purpose.

Part of her wanted to ask Carol about it, but she knew the former assistant district attorney would never divulge what had happened. It wasn't her story to tell.

After thanking Carol one more time, Sam slipped out the back door. The evening air was cooler than she had anticipated. Taking a moment to collect her thoughts, Sam looked around to make sure no one was around. While it would have been easy enough to explain why she was leaving through the back, she didn't want to have to do it. Some things were best left unsaid.

Her unmarked Ford Explorer sat underneath one of the few street lights in the public parking lot. As Sam approached it, she noticed a dark SUV with government license plates pulling off the street.

Perfect, she thought.

"I was wondering if you were ever going to come out," Gary said.

"Now you don't have to wonder." The response sounded better in her head. "Why are you still here?"

"I didn't have any place to go."

"I find that difficult to believe." Sam wondered if he had been sitting across the street waiting for her to come out of the bar.

"So what took you so long?" he asked, looking down at his watch.

"I don't see how that's any of your business." Sam was already tired of his questions. The thought of him keeping tabs on her unnerved her.

"I'm just curious why it took you five hours to come outside."

"You realize it's against the law to stalk someone,

right? Especially a police officer." Sam knew the threat was empty, but it made her feel better to say it.

"I'm not trying to start a fight," Gary said, holding up his hands in surrender. "I was just a little concerned. I thought maybe something had happened to you."

Sam didn't bother to respond to his statement. She knew if she did, it would only prolong their conversation and she needed to get away from him before she said something she would end up regretting. With a roll of her eyes, Sam proceeded to unlock her SUV and get inside. She was reaching for the start button when she saw Gary get out of his vehicle.

"Is everything okay with you?"

"It would be if you'd stop stalking me," Sam replied. The moment the words came out, she regretted saying them. He looked as if she had slapped him. "I'm sorry, I didn't mean that the way it sounded."

"It's okay." Gary took a step backward. "Have a good night, Detective."

"Gary, wait…"

It was too late. The federal agent was already in his SUV. Without looking in her direction, he pulled away, leaving two black marks in his wake.

"Smooth move," Sam said, closing her door.

For a second, she thought about sending him a text to apologize. It was the right thing to do, but she couldn't bring herself to do it.

"There's no future for us," she said, looking at herself in the rearview mirror.

Chapter 63

Christine was watering her rose bushes when Sam pulled up across the street. All signs of the mess she had created on her front lawn were gone.

Wishing she could have gone unnoticed, Sam sighed before making her way across the road. Like it or not, she had to tell her neighbor what was going on with the investigation into her daughter.

"How's it going?"

"It's going," Christine replied, shutting off the nozzle. "Just so you know, some of the other board members have asked me to resign from the homeowner's association."

That did not come as a surprise to Sam. The people

who lived in the Willowdale neighborhood valued their privacy above all else. The story of Christine's daughter murdering someone would be too much for many of them to tolerate.

"I'm sorry." The words didn't change anything, but Sam knew they had to be said. "Would you like me to talk to them?"

"I knew what I was doing. The minute I let those news vans in, I knew it would cost me my seat on the board." Christine began rolling up the hose. "At least they're not asking me to move out."

"They can't force you to leave."

"No, but they can make my life miserable if I stay." With the hose tucked away behind the flowers, Christine invited Sam in for a cup of coffee.

As they made their way into the kitchen, Sam told Christine about the arrest warrant. The news did not shock the woman.

"I always knew she'd end up in jail one day. She was always taking the easy way out. Never wanted to hold down a job or a man. It was like she was determined to ruin her life." Christine handed Sam a cup, filled to the brim with coffee. "How much time do you think they'll give her?"

"It's hard to say." Sam did not want to talk about it. "How are your other daughters taking the news?"

"As sad as it is to say, they weren't surprised either. Like I said, we've been waiting for this day for years." Christine sat down across from Sam and began stirring sugar into her drink. "The worst part of all this is they're going to have to explain to their friends why their sister is a murderer."

Sam didn't want to imagine what that was going to be like for the women. Having grown up outside of her family, she had never had to justify her father's business to any of her friends and wasn't sure how she would have handled it, had she been forced to do it.

"Megan's lawyer has been calling me all afternoon."

There's a shock, Sam thought.

"She's convinced someone is setting her up. She even brought up your name, saying you were out to get Megan back for what she did to you." Christine wiped the tears from her eyes. "I don't understand why she just doesn't confess. They found the murder weapon at her house for God's sake."

"I'm sure her lawyer will discuss all of her options once the charges are filed."

"She'll probably claim temporary insanity or something." Christine shook her head in disgust. "I just don't understand why she wants to put all of us through this. She has to know how much this is going to hurt her sisters."

Sam didn't know how to respond to the statement. In her experience, criminals never thought about how their actions affect those around them. By nature, those who broke the law were selfish. Only worried about themselves.

"I'm sorry. I don't mean to ramble on about this."

"It's okay," Sam said, reaching over to pat Christine's hand. "I can't imagine what you and your daughters are going through, but if it helps to talk about it, I'm all ears."

"You're a sweetheart, but I don't want to trouble you with my problems. We'll get through this one way or the other."

Sam admired her strength. She wasn't sure what she'd do if she were in the woman's shoes. The voice in the back of her head told her that she'd crawl into a closet somewhere and die of shame.

That ain't right. I have been dealing with this my entire life. My dad's killed more people than I can count.

The sound of her phone ringing pulled Sam away from her thoughts. Glancing at the caller ID, she excused herself.

"Good evening," Sam said, as she pulled the front door closed.

"Good evening. I was wondering if you had a little free time tonight?" Agent Thurman asked. "I wanted to talk to you about the case."

Sam looked down at her watch. The nap she had taken at the Last Call had done the trick. After weighing her options on where to meet the agent, Sam suggested they meet at L'ultima cena. Not because she cared one way or the other if their conversation was recorded. She was just in the mood for some fine Italian dining, and it didn't get any better than what Luca made.

"Do you happen to know the address off the top of

your head?"

As Sam gave her the address to the restaurant, she found herself wondering what the agent wanted to talk to her about. It wasn't like there was any question as to who had killed Aaron.

"My GPS says I can be there in twenty minutes."

"It's going to take me a little longer than that, I'm at home." Sam looked across the street at her house. "Give me an hour."

"That's fine. I'll see you there."

Chapter 64

"This place is amazing," Lisa said, staring at the large fresco of the last supper painted on the wall. "If I didn't know any better, I'd swear we were in Venice or maybe Milan." She pointed at the statue of the Virgin Mary in the corner. "Is that real marble?"

"It is," Sam said, remembering the day her father commissioned the sculpture. "Luca believes in authenticity. He modeled this place after a restaurant in Sicily."

Lisa looked around the table, then asked Sam why the hostess had refused to give them menus or offer them something to drink.

Before Sam could answer, the old Italian came over to their table with two glasses of vermouth in his hands.

"Tonight, you will think that you've died and gone to Heaven."

Sam couldn't stop herself from smiling. In spite of losing his mother, Luca seemed as jolly as ever. She suspected it was because he felt like L'ultima cena was his true home. A place where he could be himself.

"So what are we having?"

"The finest meal this side of Sicily," he answered, then winked at her. "Enjoy your aperitivo. The first course will be here before you know it."

"What's an aperitivo?" Lisa asked, smelling the liquor in her glass.

"A pre-meal drink," Sam replied, sipping her vermouth. "It's supposed to prepare your stomach for food. I think it's just an excuse to have another drink with dinner."

For the next few minutes, they chatted about how different cultures approached alcohol and its consumption, leaving Sam to believe that Lisa was setting her up for some kind of surprise. When the first course was delivered, she leaned back in her chair and told Sam that she had second thoughts about Megan's guilt.

Sam could tell the woman wasn't joking. Something had convinced the woman they had jumped the gun. Sam knew it wasn't the evidence. That meant it had something to do with how they discovered it.

What did she see?

"Have you had a chance to look over Megan's statement yet?" Lisa asked.

"I didn't know she made one." Sam cursed herself for taking the nap at the Last Call.

Lisa pulled a tablet from her purse, then slid it across the table. "Look at the part where she talks about the night Aaron went missing."

Scrolling to the middle of the first page, Sam saw what the agent was talking about. Megan stated that after she and Aaron had gone off to find a quiet spot, they had gotten into a fight about his infidelity. Sometime during the argument, Aaron had said he was done, and walked away, leaving her all alone.

"We suspected they had a fight about him cheating on her," Sam said, attempting to figure out what she was missing in the statement.

"She claims the fight took place at the lake."

"Okay. It's not like she's the first criminal who denied being at the crime scene. What makes you think she's telling the truth?"

"Look at her next statement. She lists a number of people who saw her coming out of the woods alone. How or why that never made it into the original report is beyond me."

"I can tell you why it was never mentioned."

Sam spent the next ten minutes telling the agent all about Sgt. Edwards and his lack of desire to do anything above the bare minimum. Then she explained how he had lost his job.

"Has anyone tried talking to him about this case?"

"James and Amy both tried talking to him. The man knows that as long as he keeps his mouth shut, there's nothing we can do to him."

"I take it that you looked into his whereabouts on the night Aaron went missing?"

"Of course," Sam said. "To be honest, I was kind of hoping he had killed the guy. It'd serve him right if he had to spend his retirement in a jail cell. The man's a real piece of work."

"What about the stepfather? Isn't Edwards related to him somehow?"

"Cousins. The two of them are still thick as thieves. Tim had plenty of reasons to want to hurt Aaron, but he didn't have the opportunity to do it." Sam could see her argument wasn't winning over the federal agent. "What makes you think Megan didn't kill him?"

"I'm not saying that she didn't. I'm just not as convinced as I was when she was arrested. She admits to wanting to have him locked up but swears she didn't kill him."

"What about the evidence we found at her house?" Sam asked. "How did she explain us finding the bat and watch?"

"According to her, someone must have planted the stuff." Lisa shrugged. "I know. Everyone says that when they get caught. I can't explain why I have this feeling, but my gut tells me she didn't do it."

"I wish." Sam fell silent when she watched the waiter bring their second course. She felt bad that they hadn't finished their first one. When he was gone, she explained why she had been hoping anyone other than

Megan had committed the murder.

"I didn't realize you knew her mother so well."

"I do and I don't. It's not like we're friends or anything. She's just a nice older woman who happens to live across the street from me. You'd like her. She's one of those people who would do anything for anyone."

"Did you tell her that we arrested her daughter?"

Sam nodded as the memory flashed in her mind. "She knew it was coming."

"What are her other children like?"

"I've never met them, but I know one is a cancer nurse and the other is some kind of computer programmer." Sam tapped her fingers on the table. "Hold on, that ain't right. She makes apps for a living. Something that helps people organize their schedules or something."

"You're not into the whole internet thing, are you?"

Sam leaned forward, so that she could keep her voice low. While she wasn't embarrassed by her lack of computer skills, she knew it bothered other people and she hated to make others feel uncomfortable.

"You're not the first person I've met who avoids them whenever possible. To this day, I'm not sure if we're better off having computers or not. Don't get me wrong, as a species, I think we've advanced since their invention, but we've also lost something along the way."

"Like the ability to communicate with each other?" Sam asked, feeling sorry for the world's youth. Most would never know what it was like to live without a phone or computer in their hands.

"That, and privacy. You can't stub your toe without everyone knowing about it. Twenty-five years ago you never heard of someone's identity being stolen. Now it happens a hundred times per day."

"What are you going to do? Shut it all down and go back to living in the stone ages?"

Lisa shrugged again. "If I knew the answer to that, I wouldn't be working for a living, I can tell you that."

"Speaking of working for a living, our third course is here." Sam tilted her head in the direction of the young man carrying a tray filled with bite sized slivers of meat. From where she was sitting, it looked like some kind of dried fish.

Chapter 65

Both women groaned when Luca sat a plate of fresh strawberries on the table.

"Are you trying to make me feel bad?" he asked, waving the waiter over. "Bring these two some champagne," he said to the guy.

"I'm not complaining," Lisa said, pushing the plate away, "but if I eat another bite, I'm going to explode."

"You women worry too much. Good food will solve all of your problems." Luca turned to Sam. "Non è vero?"

"If you say so." Sam looked at the strawberries, wondering if the chef would be upset if she declined to eat them. Part of her thought so. Taking the smallest one from the plate, she tossed it into her mouth.

Luca shook his head, then asked the agent if she had enjoyed her meal.

"When you said we'd think we had died and gone to Heaven, I didn't know you were being literal. You could have fed a small army with that amount of food."

The old Italian tossed his head back and laughed. "This is the problem with you Americans. You were never taught how to eat good food."

Sam reached over and squeezed his hand. "You spoil us, my friend."

"Piacere mio." He leaned to his left in order to give the waiter room to set their glasses of champagne down. "Drink up while I bring your dessert."

Like a bad dream, he was gone before either one had a chance to say a word. When Lisa asked if he was serious, Sam nodded.

"He believes every meal should come with two desserts. Don't worry, it will be something small."

"You better hope so, because you're going to have to eat two of them." The agent leaned back and patted her stomach. "That was the best food I've ever eaten in my life."

"The man does know his way around the kitchen." Sam stopped one of the waitresses as she was passing by the table. "Can you take this plate away? We're done." When they were alone, she asked Lisa what she wanted to do about their case.

"I'd like to talk to some of these people who may have seen Megan that night, but even if she's telling the truth, it doesn't explain why we found the murder weapon underneath her floor."

Sam was thinking the same thing. There could only be one reason why the baseball bat was under the house. Megan had hidden it there.

"How much do I owe you for dinner?"

"Nothing, it's on me," Sam replied, not telling the woman that Luca would never allow her to pay for a meal. "So when are you heading back to the east coast?"

"I figured that I would hang out here until we get the test results back. Just in case we're wrong."

Won't happen, Sam thought. While she couldn't be sure what the feds in the lab would find when it came to the bat, she knew what was on the watch. Skin cells taken from Megan.

"Do you have a place to stay?"

"The field office in San Francisco put me up in a hotel just this side of the bridge."

"They're making you drive back and forth between here and Sausalito?" Sam asked, wondering what kind of an idiot would think that was a good idea.

"I'm assuming they had no idea where Camden was."

"There's no way I'm letting you make that commute every day." Sam pulled her phone out and called Carol. "Can you book a suite at the Marriott for me? Put the reservation under Lisa Thurman. Thanks."

"I can't afford to stay in a suite."

"Don't worry about it, the department will pay for it. We're the one who asked you to help out with the case. The least we can do is make sure you have a nice place to lay your head down."

"Speaking of which. I should get going. My second wind is about to die out on me. I don't know how you do it. I slept on the plane and my butt is still dragging."

"I caught a power nap after I left the station." Sam

reached into her purse and pulled three hundred dollars out. While it was more than double what the meal would have cost them, she believed in tipping well. "The Marriott is over on Commerce across from the CHP barracks."

"I'm sure I'll be able to find it." Lisa extended her hand. "Thanks again for dinner. Next time, you'll have to let me treat you."

"You got it," Sam said, slipping the wad of twenties to the waiter as he came to collect their glasses. "I'll see you in the morning."

After waiting for the agent to leave, Sam made her way through the kitchen and knocked on Luca's door. The old Italian waved her in, motioning for her to sit down.

"Tell me the truth. How was your meal?"

"Delicious as always. Although you could have made the portions a little smaller. I'm stuffed. And what was the deal with offering a second dessert?"

"My mama always said you have to finish a good meal with a fine wine and something sweet to eat."

Sam bowed her head, wishing she had never asked

the question. "I'm so sorry for your loss. Is there anything I can do for you?"

"No. But thank you for offering. You've always been such a good friend to me." Luca got up and gave her a hug. "Enough with the sad talk. How are you? Have you made a decision about what you're going to do?"

"Sort of." Sam took a deep breath, hoping that she was making the right choice by telling him that she had decided to join the family. In her heart, she knew the man would be ecstatic. Like Carol, he owed everything to the Carlucci family. To him, they were nothing short of saviors. "When this case is over, I'm quitting the police department."

Chapter 66

Sam was still thinking about her decision to tell Luca about her plans as she crossed the Golden Gate Bridge into San Francisco. It was a calculated risk. Although he had promised to keep it a secret until she had a chance to tell her father, Sam knew time was of the essence.

Like all the Italians she knew, Luca loved to spread good news. It made no difference if it was about discovering a new recipe or his favorite football team winning a big game, he couldn't wait to tell others about it. Sam just hoped that he could hold out a little longer. The beep from her toll pass brought Sam back to reality.

"What am I doing?" The question hung in the air

like a bad smell.

Somewhere in the back of her mind, she felt the decision weighing on her. While she believed it was the right choice, Sam couldn't help but wonder how her life would change once she told her father.

Before anything was done, she'd have to clear everything out of her home. She didn't want the government to confiscate her belongings, meager as they were.

Would they take my stuff?

While it didn't seem likely, Sam knew it was a possibility. She had fooled them. They'd want retribution. They'd want to humiliate her and confiscating everything she owned would do that.

You're being silly.

The debate raged on as she turned into the city's most exclusive neighborhood. Seacliff was home to politicians, celebrities, and tech moguls. It was a place where the rich could show off and stay safe at the same time.

As she topped the hill, Sam spotted her father's mansion, looming over the dark ocean. While it was nowhere as large as his Windsor estate, it was still impressive. The Mediterranean architecture set it apart from its neighbors.

Slowing as she approached the gate, Sam considered changing her mind. Life as a cop wasn't so bad. She could go wherever she wanted and do whatever she wanted to do. It just took more planning. Police officers weren't supposed to throw money around like it meant nothing to them.

Stop it, she told herself. *You've made your decision. Live with it.*

When the first guard approached, Sam rolled all the windows down. They would want to look inside the car before they allowed her to proceed. As usual, the man didn't speak until he was sure no one else was inside the vehicle.

"Park near the garage," he said, before motioning to the other guard standing near the gate.

Sam brought two fingers to her forehead to acknowledge his request. Easing her foot off the brake pedal, she allowed the Subaru to inch its way past the wrought iron gate.

This is it, she told herself. *No going back now.*

The moment she brought the car to a stop, the front door of the house swung open, revealing her oldest cousin Paul. The gangster wasted no time closing the distance between her and the mansion.

"What brings you to the city?" he asked, opening her door for her.

"Good to see you too," Sam said, wishing he would take a step back to give her room to get out. "What's with the full court press?"

"You took a big risk coming here. Are you aware that your face is all over the news?" To prove his point, he pulled his phone from his pocket and showed her an image of her standing in front of the police station. "You need to be more careful. You never know who's watching."

"I know how to lose a tail," Sam responded. "This isn't my first rodeo, you know?"

"It's the first time your face has been plastered all over the news. What were you thinking?" Paul sighed as he put his phone away. "Your job is to be discreet."

Sam couldn't believe her cousin was speaking to her

as if she were a child. He knew as well as she did, that at any moment she could become his boss. With that came a certain amount of respect. Narrowing her eyes, she got out of the vehicle.

Within the blink of an eye, Paul realized his mistake. No words had been spoken, yet Sam had made her point. He was no longer in a position to question her actions or motives.

Spinning around, he escorted her to the home, making sure that he left a reasonable amount of space between her and himself. When they reached the door, he stepped to the side and allowed her to enter first. A true sign of respect.

"Il mio bambino è tornato," Anastasia said, as she raced over to where Sam was standing. "How are you doing?"

"I'm good," Sam replied, wondering why her mother was making such a fuss about her visit. "Is everything okay here?"

"Of course, why would you ask?"

Sam turned and looked at Paul. "You two are acting a little weird."

"Did you not tell her?" Anastasia asked Paul. Although he nodded, she refocused on Sam and began telling her how the news had been talking about her all night. "They're speaking about you as if you are some kind of superhero. It's not good, Samorn."

"I have no idea what you're talking about, mother. All we did was close a murder case today."

"Show her." Anastasia pointed her slender finger in the direction of the family room.

Following her cousin into the large space, Sam wondered if the whole world had gone crazy. She couldn't imagine why a twenty-four-year-old murder case in Camden would be cause for any media attention, let alone the major networks based in San Francisco. Then she remembered they had all come to her small town because she had asked them to cover the story.

What have I done? Sam asked herself, when her cousin tuned the flat screen television to the local Fox affiliate.

Chapter 67

It didn't take long for the news to cycle to the story in Camden. For the most part, it regurgitated the few facts which had been released by the department earlier in the day. An arrest had been made. The victim's family had been notified. What changed was Christine's reaction to the news that her daughter had been named as the killer. Like any parent, she apologized to the victim's family, then tried to distance herself from her bad seed.

None of it surprised Sam. It was a cookie cutter report. One which had been played throughout time all over America. What caught her attention was the news conference given by the chief after she had left the station.

After providing a few details about the case, Chief Sharp heaped all the praise upon her and her skills as a detective. Sam felt faint. In the grand scheme of things, she had played a small role in the investigation. In her opinion, James and Amy deserved most of the credit.

As her official police portrait was shown, the chief explained how Sam had broken the case wide open. While most of what he said was true, he made it sound as if she had worked alone.

Why is he doing this?

The answer came when Special Agent Lisa Thurman entered the shot. Looking like a typical federal agent, she echoed the chief's statement, giving Sam one hundred percent of the credit.

No wonder the chief is making it sound like I did all the heavy lifting.

For reasons Sam could never understand, her boss was enamored with federal law enforcement officers. In his eyes, they could do no wrong. Everything they said was the gospel truth.

Paul hit the mute button when the segment ended. "You need to speak to your father about this," he said.

Although he made it sound like a suggestion, Sam could tell that he didn't feel like there was any choice in the matter.

Not wanting to lose the ground she had gained, Sam turned and walked into the kitchen instead of heading straight to her father's office. The move was petty, but she needed to make it clear to her cousin that she moved at her own pace and would do as she chose instead of taking direction from someone beneath her station in life.

The second she rounded the corner; Sam sensed the change in herself. She was no longer acting like Sam Wright. That part of her life was over.

When her mother looked up, Sam asked her to make a cup of coffee, leaving off the word "please" as she did. Anastasia picked up on the difference immediately.

"You've made your decision." The woman shut her eyes and mumbled what sounded like a prayer.

Sam couldn't bring herself to answer her mother. She felt like she was betraying everything the woman stood for. After a brief pause, she turned and walked out of the room.

Sixty-one steps, Sam told herself. *That's all it is.*

The number of steps it took to go from the kitchen to her father's office was ingrained in her memory. At first, counting the distance had been a game. A distraction to keep her from yelling at her mother when they would fight. Sam had learned early on in life that her father's sanctuary was also her own.

Tony waved her into the room before she had a chance to knock on the open door. As usual, he had a glass of scotch sitting in front of him.

Taking a seat, Sam told her father that she had made her choice. Once the case was closed, she'd be giving up her life as Sam Wright and assume her place by his side.

The mob boss didn't speak. He just picked up his glass and took a drink. It was as if he hadn't expected her to say that she was joining the family.

"Aren't you going to say anything?" Sam asked, wishing she could read her father's mind. She had been expecting him to be overjoyed. She was fulfilling her destiny. At some point in the future, she'd be taking her rightful place at the head of the table.

"Now is not a good time, Samorn."

"What?" Sam was flabbergasted. Out of all the things she thought her father would say, "*Now is not a good time,*" wasn't among them.

"Let me explain," he said, getting up from his chair. "Have you seen the news?"

"What does that have to do with anything? You said I could take my place by your side."

"And you will. Just not today." Tony walked over and put his hand on her shoulder. "Do you have any idea what happened today?"

Sam shook her head. She didn't understand how her being in the news made any difference. Once the world found out she was really Samorn Carlucci and not Sam Wright, she'd make headlines around the world, not just in California.

"Thanks to your boss and that federal agent, everyone in this state now knows who you are. This is the moment we've been working toward."

"I have no idea what you're talking about," Sam said, wondering why her father was trying to hold her back.

"Think about it, Samorn. By solving this case,

you've become the most famous detective in California. Tomorrow morning, every agency in the state is going to want you to come work for them."

"That's not how it works." Sam had to close her eyes to keep from rolling them. "None of the big departments are going to care that I solved one murder case. It's not like I figured out who killed Kennedy."

The mob boss walked over to his desk and picked up his glass of scotch. After taking a sip of the amber liquid, he asked her to name another detective in the state who had solved a murder case in the last year.

"I have no idea," Sam said.

"That's my point. The media doesn't care about the cases that get solved, because they don't scare the general public. They're all about the killings and mayhem."

Sam had to bite her lip to keep from telling her father to get to the point. She didn't understand how someone so powerful could beat around the bush on a regular basis when it came to discussing her future.

"Why do you think they're so focused on you?" Tony asked. "Because you're different from the rest.

You're young, beautiful, and have a track record the others can only dream of."

"I'm trying hard to understand what you mean, but I don't get what you're trying to say."

"I'm saying that tomorrow morning someone from the SFPD will be calling you to ask if you want to join their department. I expect you to say yes."

Chapter 68

Sam wanted to scream. All of her hopes and dreams were vanishing before her eyes. Instead of taking over the last major crime family in existence, she was going to be stuck being a cop. All because her father wanted a Carlucci to head the SFPD.

Tony sensed her disappointment. He explained that her remaining a detective would only be temporary. Just long enough for him to convince the other families that it would be okay for a woman to take over for him.

"Then why did you give me the choice?" Sam asked.

"I'm not taking away your choice. You will still be able to take your place in this family, just not today. I don't understand why you are so upset about this. A few weeks ago, you were happy being a cop. What changed?"

"I…" Sam didn't know how to answer the question. From the moment she learned she had a choice; she had been looking for an excuse to remain a cop. Unlike her family, the police made a positive difference in the world. They helped people.

"We'll talk about it more this weekend."

"But…" Sam knew that she was being dismissed. Standing up, she kissed her father on the cheek, then told him that she'd see him in a few days.

Sam didn't waste any time leaving the house. It was the first time in her life she had left without saying goodbye to her mother. She knew she'd pay for it later. Her only saving grace was that she knew no one would contact her before the weekend.

All the way back to Camden, Sam thought about her father's decision to make her continue as Sam Wright. It felt wrong, but she knew he had a reason for doing what he did. While she may not understand it, there was no way she was going to question it. When the SFPD called in the morning, she would do as she was told.

I wonder how the others are going to take it.

Sam could picture Jenna and the others being happy for her. If given the chance, any one of them would leave Camden in a heartbeat.

So why am I so mad about it?

No matter how hard she tried to come up with an answer, Sam kept drawing a blank. There was no reason for her to be upset. From the moment of her birth, the plan had been for her to end up leading a big department like the SFPD.

Shaking the thought from her head, she called Jenna. In spite of the late hour, she knew the sergeant would be awake.

"What's up?"

"How come no one told me that my face was going to be plastered all over the news?" Sam asked, trying to make it sound like it didn't bother her.

"Sorry about that. I was planning on telling you about it. But the interview with Megan ran long. By the time I left the station, I had forgotten all about it."

"How are James and Amy taking it?" Sam could picture the two detectives complaining about how she always got all the attention.

"They know it wasn't your idea to hog all the credit. By the way, can you tell your neighbor to dial it down a bit? Marsha has called me fifteen times complaining about her being on the news."

The memory of seeing Christine standing in her front yard talking with a reporter popped into Sam's mind. "I'll do what I can."

"Thanks." Jenna paused for a few seconds. "You did good, Sam. We wouldn't have closed this one without you."

"Just doing my job. Can you make sure James and Amy get something in their file. They worked as many hours as I did."

"I'll take care of it. One more thing. We got a report back from the lab. The feds matched the hair and blood found on the bat to Aaron. It's definitely the murder weapon."

"I guess that's it then." Sam knew the evidence pulled from the bat would put Megan away for life. It was a fitting end to the story. Her only regret was that she had wasted her time chasing down the stolen watch.

"Yep. Marsha said there won't be any plea bargain

in this case."

"Not even if she pleads guilty?" Sam asked.

"Marsha said it won't make any difference. Now that we have the murder weapon, there's no reason not to go for the max."

"Makes sense." Sam started to thank God for letting them find the bat when something stirred in her mind. "Did anyone mention that we found the bat when we searched her home?"

"Not that I know of, why?"

"I could have sworn someone mentioned it to me earlier." Sam fell silent as she tried to remember who had brought up the murder weapon.

"Was it Agent Thurman?" Jenna asked. "I heard you two had dinner together."

"Are there any secrets left in this town?"

"None worth keeping," the sergeant replied. "Get some sleep, Detective. You've earned it."

Sam thanked her boss for the kind words, then hung up the phone. That nagging voice in the back of her mind kept telling her that she was forgetting something important.

Chapter 69

"Mrs. Johnson. Your attorney has informed me that you'd like to change your plea."

"Yes, Your Honor," Megan said, wiping the tears from her eyes. "Without admitting any guilt, I'd like to change my plea to guilty."

The judge looked over at Marsha and asked her if she was willing to accept the Alford plea.

"The state has no objection, Your Honor."

Sam wasn't surprised the defendant had chosen to throw herself on the mercy of the court. The evidence against her was overwhelming. Looking over her shoulder, Sam spotted Christine standing in the back of the courtroom. The retired nurse had a strange look of satisfaction written all over her face.

"Pay attention," Jenna said, elbowing Sam in the ribs.

With the guilty plea accepted, the judge sentenced Megan to twenty-five years to life.

An audible gasp was heard through the courtroom. Again, Sam was not surprised. Given the evidence, there was no reason to go easy on the woman.

As the bailiff escorted Megan through the side door, Marsha turned and thanked the federal agents sitting behind her. It was their testimony that had sealed the deal. That and the DNA recovered from the bat.

"What's wrong with you?" Jenna asked. "We won."

Sam turned and watched Christine leave the room. Something was off. The woman no longer looked like the grieving mother.

"Excuse me for a minute." Racing out of the courtroom, Sam caught up with Christine just as she was about to board the elevator. "How are you doing?"

"I'm glad it's over," the woman said. "I just wish she wouldn't have dragged it out this long. She should have pleaded guilty the minute you guys found the bat."

The statement hit Sam like a ton of bricks. It was similar to what she had said to her the night they had completed the search of Megan's home.

"Oh my God. You did it. You killed Aaron."

The end…

If you like this book, please consider leaving a review on Amazon or Goodreads.

And please keep turning the pages as I share my thoughts on this book.

About the story

This story was an absolute blast to write. Sam's evolution constantly surprises me. Each time I expect her to do something, she goes off in a different direction.

I've been asked if Sam will give up her life as Sam Wright, and the answer is, I'm not sure. Part of me thinks so, but if it happens, it won't be any time soon. I'm enjoying her life as a detective. I can say that one day in the very near future, her secret will be exposed.

Until next time…

About the author

Sterling Kirkland grew up in the shadow of Washington D.C. where he began writing short stories at age eleven. When not crafting a new story, he can be found reading horror, thriller and fantasy books or hanging out with the local Corvette and Mustang car clubs at regional car shows.

sterlingkirkland.com

facebook.com/sterlingkirkland

bookbub.com/authors/sterling-kirkland

goodreads.com/sterlingkirkland

Other books by Sterling Kirkland

The Haunted Witch (The Witches of Heartstone)

Rise of the Necromancer (The Witches of Heartstone)

Merging Realms (A Jessie Winters novella)

Counted Sorrows (A Jessie Winters novella)

The New Protocol (A Mike Black thriller)

The Lost Protocol (A Mike Black thriller)

The Promotion (The Mafia's Detective)

Hard Choices (The Mafia's Detective)

Last Call (The Mafia's Detective)

Coming soon

Past Mistakes (The Mafia's Detective)

Open Secrets (The Mafia's Detective)

Golden Pines (A psychological Thriller)

The Pilot's Gamble (A Lost Treasure Mystery)

The Peddler's Gold (A Lost Treasure Mystery)

The Banker's Account (A Lost Treasure Mystery)

The Author's Challenge (A Lost Treasure Mystery)

The Soldier's Cache (A Lost Treasure Mystery)

The Niner's Promise (A Lost Treasure Mystery)